U0093984

哈福

哈福

哈福

可以馬上學會的

超強

最有效率的口說訓練法
破解口說密碼、突破瓶頸

英語口說課

一次搞定：TOEIC．TOEFL．IELTS．英檢．學測．會考

附
MP3

蘇盈盈・珊朵拉 —— 合著

哈福

最有效率的口說訓練法
破解口說密碼、突破瓶頸

一次搞定：TOEIC、TOEFL、IELTS、英檢、學測、會考

　　隨著國際化的快速趨勢，為了跟上潮流，學好國際第一通用外語－英語，就是大家眼前最重要的功課。學英語的好處很多：除了可以開拓自己的眼界、結交更多朋友、獲得多元的第一手消息、瀏覽網站更方便等，影響我們最大的，無非是精通英語在職場上佔盡的優勢！想進國際化的大公司，不會英語那就真是 No way 了！

　　學語言，除了希望可以閱讀、欣賞他國文化外，最希望的當然還是能說出流利道地的外文，跟外國人輕鬆溝通囉！為了讓讀者有更親切的學習環境，本公司特別編撰「超強英語」系列，強力增進您的英語能力。書加 MP3 雙管齊下，讓您彈指翻閱之間，英語實力馬上提升；加上 MP3 的強力放送，讓自己無時不泡「英語澡」，保證流利英語迅速脫口說！

　　本書分為五章，每章約十個單元，內容為道地美國學生的生活實況會話，從租屋、學業、乾洗經驗、購物、開戶、提款、水電問題、選購生日禮物、休閒、音樂、電影到交通相關狀況，完整收錄。

　　想流暢地用英語表達生活相關話題，侃侃而談週遭的日常新鮮事，本系列是您不可或缺的最佳幫手！

本系列最大特色：

1 原汁原味‧美語會話：

為呈現原汁原味的美語會話，特聘請英語教材專家撰寫，內容自然生活化，用字簡單，情境逼真，故事輕鬆，看完實力馬上突飛猛進！

2 句型簡潔‧方便套用：

年輕的角色對話，新鮮流行的校園話題，讀完可以馬上跟英語同好沙盤演練一番，英語口說聽力絕對一把罩！

3 嚴謹編撰‧專業錄音：

由美籍專業播音員，精心錄製的精質 MP3，發音純正標準，腔調自然符合情境，讓您在實況會話的帶領下，快速學會道地美式發音。

4 實況對話‧流利逼真：

本書特地營造出最佳英語環境，把英語帶進生活圈，做個聽、說皆棒的「國際人」。本書讓您時時說英語，日日是好日。與人對答如流、實力大躍進！

　　隨書附贈一片 MP3，實況模擬，專業錄音，搭配學習，效果加倍！

編者　謹識

CONTENTS

Home Sweet Home! 甜蜜的家

Out and About 出門在外

Chapter 5

That's Entertainment 那才是娛樂

Chapter 1

That's What Friends Are For

朋友的意義

Life isn't about what you study in school, or what kind of job you do. It's not about your grades or how much money you make, either. What makes life worth living is one's friends and family. In this book you'll meet a group of friends—students at Vancouver University—and their families. Although they all care about school and work, what they care most about is each other—after all, that's what friends are for!

人生並不只是你在學校的課業，或職場上的工作而已。它也不等於你的考試成績或是和你賺得的財富。在你一生中最重要的，是你所結交的朋友和你的家人。您將在本書中遇到一群朋友——溫哥華大學學生及他們的家人。雖然他們也都很在乎課業及工作，但是他們最在意的還是對方——因為畢竟這是朋友的可貴之處。

Unit 1

Staying in Touch

保持聯絡

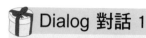Track-2

 Dialog 對話 1

Megan is talking to her friend Paul about moving to a new city.
梅格正在和她的朋友保羅談起要遷往新的都市。

P   : I'm sure going to miss you, Megan.
保羅 : 我一定會想念你的，梅格。

M   : I'll miss you too, Paul. Make sure you stay in touch.
梅格 : 我也會想念你，保羅。你一定要和我保持聯絡喲！

P   : Of course! I've got your new phone number, so I can call you whenever I feel lonely.
保羅 : 當然，我有你的新電話，只要我感到孤單，就可以打電話給你。

M   : And I've got your email address in case I want to drop you a line.
梅格 : 如果我想要寫信給你，我也有你的新電子郵件住址。

P   : That reminds me! What's your email address?
保羅 : 你這番話提醒了我！你的電子郵件住址是什麼？

M : Megan-ninety-nine at coolmail-dot-com. But, please, don't tell anyone else.

梅格 : Megan99@coolmail.com。但是，拜託，請別跟別人說！

P : Why not?

保羅 : 為什麼不要説？

M : This account is only for my close friends—I don't want it to be full of junk mail!

梅格 : 這個帳號僅和我要好的朋友保持聯絡用的—我不希望信箱塞滿了垃圾郵件！

🎁 Dialog 對話 2

Megan and Paul continue their conversation.
梅格和保羅繼續交談著。

M : To tell you the truth, Paul, I'm a little worried about losing touch with you guys.

梅格 : 老實説，保羅，我有點擔心和你失去聯絡。

P : You don't have to worry about us. I'd be more worried about you making so many new friends you'll forget all about us!

保羅 : 你不用擔心我們。反倒是我還比較擔心你因為結交了許多新朋友，會把我們全都給忘了！

M　　：Well, I hope I'll make new friends, but I'm not sure how I'll meet new people.

梅格　：我希望自己結交新朋友，但是我不確定如何認識新朋友。

P　　：I'm sure you'll have lots in common with your new classmates; and if you join a club at school, then you'll make friends fast.

保羅　：我相信，你會和你的新同學發現許多共通之處，而且如果你加入學校社團，很快就會交到新朋友

M　　：That's great idea. But actually, I was hoping you could give me your cousin's number. Grant goes to Vancouver University too, right?

梅格　：這建議不錯。只不過，事實上，我希望你能讓我知道你表哥的電話號碼。格蘭也在溫哥華大學就讀，對吧？

P　　：Right! I'm sure he'd be happy to show you around and introduce you to some of the people he knows.

保羅　：沒錯！我相信他會樂於帶你四處看看，把他所認識的一些朋友介紹給你。

M　　：I'll have plenty of friends in no time!

梅格　：沒多久我就會結交許多朋友了！

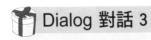 Dialog 對話 3

Paul and Megan are about ready to say their goodbyes.

保羅和梅格準備互道珍重。

P : Well, I guess that's about everything. All your boxes and suitcases are in the car.

保羅 : 我想該收拾的都收好了！你全部的箱子和行李箱都放進車子裡了！

M : I've turned off the lights, locked the door … you'll give my keys to my landlord?

梅格 : 我已經關好電燈，鎖好了門…你會把我的鑰匙交給我房東吧？

P : I won't forget.

保羅 : 我不會忘記的。

M : That's about everything.

梅格 : 沒什麼事要交代了！

P : Are you sure you're not forgetting anything?

保羅 : 你確定沒有遺漏些什麼吧？

M : Hmm. Yes! There's one thing I forgot!

梅格 : 嗯！有！我還忘了一件事。

P : Which is…?

保羅 : 什麼事…？

M 　　: To thank you and give you a big kiss goodbye!

梅格　　: 忘了謝謝你，以及和你吻別。

Useful Sentences 範例句型

Stay in touch!

　　保持聯絡！

Don't be a stranger!

　　不要這麼冷淡！

Have a safe trip!

　　一路平安！

Good luck in your future endeavors!

　　祝你好運！

Vocabulary 單字片語

☑		
☑ **email address**		電子郵件網址
☑ **email account**		電子郵件帳號
☑ **introduce**		介紹
☑ **plenty**		許多
☑ **suitcase**		小型旅行箱
☑ **landlord**		房東

Making New Friends
結交新朋友

🔘 Track-3

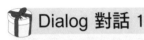 Dialog 對話 1

Megan introduces herself to a boy in her Geography class.

梅格上地理課時，跟一位男孩自我介紹。

M : Hi! My name is Megan.

梅格 : 嗨！我是梅格。

H : Mine's Harry.

哈利 : 我是哈利。

M : Nice to meet you. Are you a first-year student, too?

梅格 : 很高興認識你。你也念一年級嗎？

H : I am! Did my nervous look give me away?

哈利 : 我是！我緊張的樣子全寫在臉上嗎？

M : Nope—just a lucky guess! Listen, I was wondering, would it be okay if I asked you for your phone number or email address? That way if I miss a class, or have a question, then I'll have someone to ask.

梅格	: 不是一我只是剛好猜對罷了！我在想，如果我向你要你的電話或電子郵件信箱，會不會太冒昧？這樣一來，要是我缺課或有任何問題，就可以找到人詢問了！

H	: Great idea—but only if I can have yours, too.
哈利	: 這主意不錯一只不過你也要給我你的電子信箱。

M	: Fair enough. Do you have a pen?
梅格	: 很公平。你有帶筆嗎？

 Dialog 對話 2

Megan has joined an intramural sports club. She is resting on a bench after playing some basketball and a boy named Kurt begins to talk to her.

梅格已經加入了校內的運動社。打完籃球後，她正在椅凳上休息。一位叫做科特的男孩正要和她交談。

K	: You were pretty hot out on the court! Are you on the varsity team?
科特	: 你在球場上的表現很出色！你是不是代表隊的球員？

M	: No, I just like playing for fun.
梅格	: 不是，我就只是喜歡打著玩的。

K	: Well, you should think about trying out for the team. You've got some great moves!
科特	: 那麼，你應該考慮加入代表隊。你有些動作很不錯。

M : Thanks! How come I haven't seen you on the court yet?

梅格 : 謝了！為什麼沒看見你上球場呢？

K : I hurt my knee a few weeks ago and it hasn't healed yet. But luckily, I enjoy watching.

科特 : 我的膝蓋幾星期前受了傷，到現在都還沒痊癒。幸好，我也很喜歡當觀眾。

M : You'd make a good cheerleader!

梅格 : 你會是個一流的啦啦隊長。

K : And you'd make a good comedian! Hey, it looks like one of your teammates needs you to fill in for them.

科特 : 那麼你會是個不錯的喜劇演員。嘿！好像你的一位隊員要你去補位。

M : Looks like it. It was nice talking to you.

梅格 : 好像是這樣。和你聊天真愉快。

K : Nice talking to you, too! Maybe we can go and get a coffee after the game.

科特 : 我也很高興和你聊天。打完球後或許我們可以一起去喝杯咖啡。

M : I'd like that.

梅格 : 我很樂意。

🎁 Dialog 對話 3

Megan is home alone on Friday night and decides to give Paul's cousin, Grant, a phone call.

週五晚上，梅格獨自待在家裡，她決定打電話給保羅的表哥格蘭。

M : Hello. May I please speak to Grant Smith?

梅格 : 哈囉！請找格蘭史密斯聽電話。

G : Speaking.

格蘭 : 我就是。

M : Hi Grant. My name is Megan—I'm a friend of your cousin Paul. He gave me your number.

梅格 : 嗨！格蘭。我是梅格―是你的表弟保羅的朋友。他給了你你的電話。

G : That's right! Paul told me to expect a call from you! How are you adjusting to university life?

格蘭 : 對啊！保羅要我等你打電話來。你的大學生活適應得怎麼樣了？

M : So far, so good. I'm enjoying my classes and I've made some new friends. But I am having a little trouble finding my way around. It's so easy to get lost around here!

梅格 : 到目前為止，還不錯。我喜歡我那一班，也結交了一些新朋友。但是不太認得路，所以一不小心就會在這裡迷路。

G　　：It can be difficult to get around. If you have some free time this weekend, I'd be happy to show you around a bit.

格蘭　：這附近的路不太好認。要是你這個週末有空，我很樂意帶你四處走走。

M　　：That would be great!

梅格　：這樣就太好了！

Useful Sentences 範例句型

Allow me to introduce myself.

容我自我介紹。

I'm going to try out for the team.

我打算進校隊。

May I leave a message?

我可以留言嗎？

It was a pleasure meeting you!

認識你真好！

Vocabulary 單字片語

☑	geography	地理
☑	first-year student	一年級
☑	nervous	緊張
☑	wonder	想知道；覺得奇怪
☑	intramural sports	校內運動
☑	varsity	代表隊
☑	cheerleader	啦啦隊
☑	comedian	喜劇演員
☑	adjust	適應
☑	show somebody around	帶某人四處逛逛

MEMO

Dialog 對話 1

Grant has just given Megan a tour of the campus.

格蘭帶著梅格逛校園。

G : …and last but not least, the student union building!

格蘭 : …終於是學生活動中心！

M : I've never heard of that major.

梅格 : 我從不曾聽過這個主修科目。

G : It's not an area of study! The student union building is a space for students. There are offices for the different clubs, a space for student events, a restaurant and a coffee shop.

格蘭 : 這不是學科的一種。學生活動中心是學生專屬的空間。那裡有各種不同社團的辦公室；是一處供作學生活動、餐廳、咖啡廳的空間。

M : So it's a place for students to hang out.

梅格 : 所以，是學生打發時間的地方。

G　　　: Exactly. It's a great place to come and meet your friends, chat, or study.

格蘭　　: 沒錯。也是來與朋友會面、聊天、或唸書的好地方。

M　　　: It definitely sounds more fun than the library!

梅格　　: 這地方聽起來絕對比圖書館還有意思。

G　　　: Come on! Let's go inside and take a look around.

格蘭　　: 來吧！咱們進去裡面瞧一瞧。

 Dialog 對話 2

Grant and Megan go into the student union building's coffee shop. They sit down to enjoy a coffee.

格蘭和梅格走進學生活動中心的咖啡廳。他們坐下來享受咖啡的滋味。

G　　　: How's your coffee?

格蘭　　: 你的咖啡味道如何？

M　　　: It's OK. But I think I might have put too much sugar in it, and yours?

梅格　　: 還可以。但是我想我加了太多糖在裡面了！你的呢？

G　　　: It's great. Cappuccino is my favorite!

格蘭　　: 很不錯，我最愛喝卡布奇諾。

M　　　: Your cousin Paul likes cappuccino, too.

梅格　　: 你表弟保羅也喜歡喝卡布奇諾。

G : I guess it must run in the family!

格蘭 : 我猜這一定是家族遺傳！

M : That's not the only thing. Have I told you yet how much you and Paul look alike?

梅格 : 還不只有這一點而已！我有說過你跟保羅很像嗎？

G : That's what everyone says! But neither Paul nor I see it.

格蘭 : 大家都這麼說！但是保羅和我都沒發現。

 Dialog 對話 3

Megan and Grant have finished their coffee. They go outside and stand on the steps of the student union building.

梅格和格蘭喝完咖啡。他們走出去，站在學生活動中心的階梯上。

M : So, where else do students like to hang out?

梅格 : 那麼，學生還喜歡在其他哪些地方打發時間？

G : Well, the library is a popular spot!

格蘭 : 圖書館是人氣指數很高的地方。

M : During midterms and final exams, I'll bet.

梅格 : 我打賭一定是在期中考及期末考期間，才會如此。

G　　　: You catch on quickly! Lots of students spend time in their dormitory rooms and visit back and forth.

格蘭　　: 你蠻進入狀況的！很多學生都待在宿舍裡；並在宿舍及圖書館之間來來去去的。

M　　　: It must get pretty noisy in the dorms. Is that where you live?

梅格　　: 宿舍裡一定很吵。你是住在宿舍裡嗎？

G　　　: Yep! If you like, I can show you around.

格蘭　　: 是的！你如果有興趣，我可以帶你四處看看。

M　　　: Thanks! I'd love to see what on-campus living is like!

梅格　　: 謝啦！我的確想要知道校園生活的風貌！

Useful Sentences 範例句型

Let's hang out sometime.

我們找個時間一起去晃晃。

I want to take a look around.

我想要四處看一看。

Good looks and talent must run in your family!

美貌及才華一定是你們的家族遺傳。

Thomas was quick to catch on to the joke.

湯瑪士很快就聽懂這個笑話。

Vocabulary 單字片語

☑ campus   校園

☑ student union building   學生活動中心

☑ major   主修

☑ cappuccino   卡布奇諾

☑ midterm   期中考

☑ dormitory/dorm   宿舍

MEMO

....

....

....

....

....

....

....

....

Unit 4

Common Interests

共同的興趣

 Dialog 對話 1

Grant and Megan are walking over to Grant's dorm.

葛蘭和梅格正朝著格蘭的宿舍走去。

G   : So what are you going to major in?

格蘭 : 所以，你打算主修什麼學科？

M   : I haven't decided yet. My parents want me to study business, but I'm really interested in history and literature.

梅格 : 我還決定好。我爸媽要我學商，但我真正有興趣的科目卻是歷史及文學。

G   : Really? Me too! Who's your favorite writer?

格蘭 : 真的嗎？我也是！誰是你最喜歡的作家？

M   : That's a hard one. I have so many!

梅格 : 這個問題很難回答，因為我喜歡的作家很多！

G   : My favorite writer is George Eliot. You know, the guy who wrote Middlemarch? He's amazing!

格蘭 : 我最喜歡的作家是喬治艾略特。你知道那傢伙寫了「米德鎮的春天」嗎？他真是太棒了！

M   : You're hilarious! You're even funnier than Paul!

梅格   : 你很會耍寶！你比保羅還好笑！

G   : Er, thanks. But what's so funny about liking George Eliot?

格蘭   : 呃，謝啦！但是喜歡喬治艾略特有這麼好笑嗎？

M   : George Eliot was the pen name of a female author. It's she, not he!

梅格   : 喬治艾略特是一位女性作家的筆名。所以請用女性的「她」！

Dialog 對話 2

Megan asks Grant if he plays any sports.
梅格問格蘭是否做任何的運動。

G   : No. That's one area where Paul and I differ :
         He is very athletic, whereas I am not.

格蘭   : 沒有。這正是我和保羅不同的地方：他熱愛運動；但我不是。

M   : Yeah, Paul does love sports! He's on the rugby team, the basketball team, the hockey team...

梅格   : 是啊！保羅的確熱愛運動。他加入了足球隊、籃球隊、曲棍球隊…

G   : I know, I know! How about you? Do you play any sports?

格蘭   : 我知道，我知道！那麼你呢？你是否參加任何的球隊？

| M | : | Yes. I love to get out an exercise, but I'm not a very talented athlete. I just play intramurals. |
| 梅格 | : | 是的。我喜歡外出運動。但我沒有運動細胞,我只加入校內的團隊。 |

| G | : | Do you like watching sports? |
| 格蘭 | : | 你喜歡看運動比賽嗎? |

| M | : | Do I? I love watching basketball on TV. |
| 梅格 | : | 我喜歡嗎?我愛看電視轉播的籃球賽。 |

| G | : | Me too! Do you like the Houston Rockets? |
| 格蘭 | : | 我也是!你喜歡休斯頓火箭隊嗎? |

| M | : | I do! And Yao Ming happens to be my favorite player! |
| 梅格 | : | 我喜歡!而姚明正好就是我在喜歡的球員! |

 Dialog 對話 3

Grant and Megan are in sight of his dorm at Vancouver University.
葛蘭和梅格正在溫哥華大學的宿舍裡。

| M | : | It must be nice living up here with all the beautiful scenery. |
| 梅格 | : | 住在這兒到處都是美景的地方,一定很不錯。 |

| G | : It is. But sometimes I get a little bored. |
| 格蘭 | : 的確如此。但是有時候我覺得有點無聊。 |

| M | : What do you like to do for fun? |
| 梅格 | : 你喜歡做什麼消遣？ |

| G | : Well, when I get the chance, I like to go and watch movies. I see about one a week. |
| 格蘭 | : 有時間的話，我喜歡去看電影。我大約一週去看一場電影。 |

| M | : You know, you and I have a lot in common. I love watching movies, too! |
| 梅格 | : 你知道嗎？我們倆有許多共同的地方，我也喜歡看電影！ |

| G | : Really? Next Friday I'm planning on going to see the new Jet Li flick. Would you care to join me? |
| 格蘭 | : 真的嗎？下星期五我打算去看李連杰的新片。你要跟我去嗎？ |

| M | : It would be my pleasure! What time do you want to pick me up? |
| 梅格 | : 榮幸之至！你何時來接我？ |

Useful Sentences 範例句型

They have a lot in common.

他們有許多共同之處。

We differ in several ways: You are tall and blond, whereas I am short and have brown hair.

我們有一些地方不同：你是金髮、高挺；但是我卻是棕髮、矮小。

Do you have any talents?

你是否有任何的才能？

For fun, I like to watch movies.

我喜歡看電影打發時間。

Vocabulary 單字片語

☑ hilarious	愉悅的
☑ business	商業
☑ history	歷史
☑ literature	文學
☑ amazing	驚人的
☑ pen name	筆名
☑ scenery	風景
☑ flick	電影

Unit 5

Gossip

八卦

 Track-6

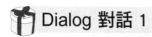 Dialog 對話 1

Grant's roommate, Josh, is talking to his classmate, Celia.

格蘭的室友賈許正在和他的同學莎莉亞交談。

C　　: So, what's the latest news down at the dorm?

莎莉亞 : 宿舍裡最近流傳什麼八卦消息？

J　　: Oh, same old thing.

喬許　: 噢！還不是同樣的老話題。

C　　: That's not what I hear!

莎莉亞 : 和我所聽到的不一樣。

J　　: Then you can fill me in. What's happening?

喬許　: 那麼你可以讓我也一起加入。發生了什麼事？

C　　: Well, Susan heard from Patricia that Janet's boyfriend told Ryan that...

莎莉亞 : 蘇珊從派翠莎那裡聽說，珍娜的男友告訴羅恩…

J　　: Can you just tell me in plain English, please?

喬許　: 能否請你用簡單的英語告訴我，好嗎？

31

C : Fine. Your roommate has a girlfriend!

莎莉亞 ： 沒問題。你的室友交了一位女朋友！

 Dialog 對話 2

Josh has just finished laughing over the possibility of Grant having a girlfriend.

喬許才剛取笑格蘭竟然有可能交上了女朋友。

J : That's a good one Celia! I think I would know if my own roommate was seeing somebody.

喬許 ： 那可是好消息，莎莉亞。但我想如果我的室友和別人約會，我應該會知道。

C : Well, he is. He's dating my friend Megan. They've been going out for a few weeks now.

莎莉亞 ： 他是啊！他是正在和我的朋友梅格約會。他們已經約會好幾星期了！

J : I guess I'm not surprised. He's rarely home … but I just thought that he had been putting in extra hours at the library.

喬許 ： 我一點也不驚訝！他很少在家，只不過我以為他多花些時間待在圖書館裡。

C : Wrong again! Grant and Megan have been spending a lot of time watching movies at the MTV!

莎莉亞 ： 你又錯了！格蘭和梅格已經有一段時間一起在 MTV 看電影了！

J : I guess with a roommate like me who's always home, Grant needs a little privacy!

喬許 : 大概是我這種不出門的室友害的,格蘭需要一點約會的隱私。

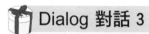 Dialog **對話** 3

Grant runs into Celia on his way out of the library.

格蘭步出圖書館時,遇到了莎莉亞。

C : Hey! What are you doing here? I'm surprised you're not at the MTV!

莎莉亞 : 嗨!你在這裡幹麻?我很訝異你沒去 MTV。

G : Huh? I don't get it.

格蘭 : 嗯?我聽不懂你說什麼!

C : Come on, you don't need to be shy! Everybody knows.

莎莉亞 : 少來了!你用不著害羞!大家都知道的。

G : Everybody knows what?

格蘭 : 大家都知道什麼?

C : About you and Megan ... dating. Admit it, you're an item.

莎莉亞 : 知道你和梅格…. 正在約會。承認吧!你已經上頭條了!

G ： I'm not sure where you got your "facts" from, Celia. But Megan and I are just good friends. Besides—I already have a girlfriend.

格蘭 ： 莎莉亞，我不知道你從哪聽來的「事實」。但是梅格和我只是好朋友而已，再說─我已經有女朋友了！

C ： Really? I didn't know that!

莎莉亞 ： 真的嗎？我不知道耶！

G ： But I have a feeling that soon everybody will...

格蘭 ： 但是我感覺很快的大家都會…

Useful Sentences 範例句型

Have you heard the news?

你聽到消息了嗎？

Kim is going out with Jordan.

吉姆和喬登約會了。

Kim and Jordan are an item.

吉姆和喬登成了新聞人物。

You should get your facts straight.

你應該直接去發掘事情的真相。

Vocabulary 單字片語

☑ fill somebody in   讓某人加入

☑ possibility   可能性

☑ in plain English   用簡單的英語

☑ be an item   成了新聞人物

☑ admit   承認

☑ privacy   隱私權

MEMO

....

....

....

....

....

....

....

....

....

....

....

Unit 6

Fair-weather Friends
泛泛之交

 Dialog 對話 1

Megan and Kurt, her varsity intramurals teammate, are having lunch together.
梅格和她的校內運動代表隊的隊友科特一起共進午餐。

M : You've got to show me how to improve my backhand swing in badminton sometime.

梅格 : 你改天一定得告訴我，如何改進我在打羽毛球時反手拍的動作。

K : I'd be glad to. How about next Saturday? Are you free?

科特 : 我很樂意。下禮拜六如何？你有空嗎？

M : I am. But the badminton courts usually aren't…

梅格 : 有空，但是羽毛球場就不一定了。

K : You're right. They can be pretty busy on the weekends. How about we practice tonight?

科特 : 你說得對，週末可能很多人。那我們今晚練習如何？

M : Sure, I don't have anything else to do.

梅格 : 當然可以，反正我也沒事做。

K : Great! I'll see you at the court at eight!

科特 : 太好了！我們八點球場見。

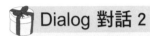 Dialog 對話 2

It's eight fifteen, and Megan is waiting at the court for Kurt. It's raining out. Finally, her phone rings.

現在是八點十五分，梅格正在球場等科特。外面正在下雨，終於，她的電話響了。

K : Megan? It's Kurt.

科特 : 梅格嗎？我是科特。

M : Hey! Are you OK? Did you have car trouble?

梅格 : 嘿！你還好吧？你的車子出問題了嗎？

K : Umm. No. Actually, since it's raining, I decided to cancel.

科特 : 嗯！事實上，不是。因為下雨了！所以我決定取消打球。

M : Oh.

梅格 : 噢！

K : I hope you don't mind. I just thought that it wouldn't be much fun. We'll do it some other time though.

科特 : 希望你不要介意。我只是想，現在打球可能不會很有趣。改天再約吧！

M	: When the weather is nicer?
梅格	: 等到天氣比較好時嗎？

K	: Exactly.
科特	: 對。

 Dialog 對話 3

Meanwhile, back at the dorm, Grant has just gotten off the phone with his girlfriend from his hometown. The phone rings immediately after and he picks it up.

回到寢室時，格蘭正掛上他女朋友的電話。電話聲一響，格蘭馬上接起來。

G	: Helen? Thank goodness you called me back! It was all a big mistake! I never meant to...
格蘭	: 海倫？感謝老天你再打電話回來！這完全是個大錯誤！我完全無意…

C	: Mmm, Grant? This isn't Helen. It's Celia. Remember me? Your good friend?
莎莉亞	: 嗯，格蘭？我不是海倫；我是莎莉亞？還記得嗎？是你的好朋友？

G	: Oh, Celia, sorry. I was just on the phone with my girlfriend and we had an argument. She thinks I'm seeing someone else!
格蘭	: 噢，莎莉亞。很抱歉。我剛和我的女朋友講電話，我們有些爭吵。她以為我和別人約會。

C : That's too bad. Listen, Grant, you're getting good grades in history, right? Would you mind helping me study for the midterm?

莎莉亞 : 真是太糟了！格蘭，你的歷史成績一向不錯，對吧？你可以幫我準備歷史期中考嗎？

G : I have an idea. Will you come over here and give me some advice about what I should do about Helen.

格蘭 : 我有個主意。你能不能來我這兒，給我一些和海倫相處的建議？

C : Sorry, Grant, but I'm pretty busy. And if you won't help me with my midterm, then I've got a lot of studying to do. Bye!

莎莉亞 : 很抱歉！格蘭。我很忙。如果你不幫我準備期中考，那我還有很多書要念。再見！

Useful Sentences 範例句型

How about we go to the museum next weekend?

我們下週末去博物館如何？

Do you think Martha will mind if I borrow her car?

你認為瑪莎會不會介意我們向她借車？

I will do my homework immediately after I go to the store.

我去了商店回來後，就會馬上做功課。

Matthew gave me some good advice to solve my problem.

馬修提供我一些建議，幫助我解決我的問題。

Vocabulary 單字片語

☑ badminton	羽毛球
☑ court	球場
☑ trouble	問題
☑ cancel	取消
☑ immediately	立即；馬上
☑ argument	爭論；爭吵
☑ midterm	期中考
☑ advice	建議

MEMO

Breaking Up is
Hard to Do

分手是件難事

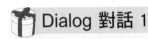 Track-8

🎁 Dialog 對話 1

Grant's girlfriend, Helen, comes to campus. The two are walking around.

格蘭的跟女友海倫來到校園，四處走走。

H	: So will you please tell me the truth about what's going on with you? I've heard so many rumors ...
海倫	: 你能不能老實告訴我，你是怎麼回事？我已經聽說許多次…

G	: And none of them are true, I swear!
格蘭	: 全都不是真的，我發誓！

H	: It's hard for me to believe.
海倫	: 我簡直不敢相信。

G	: I know, I understand. But Helen...
格蘭	: 我知道，我了解。但是，海倫…

H	: Grant. I think we should break up. I'm sorry.
海倫	: 格蘭，我想我們應該分手。很抱歉。

G　　　: I don't know what to say.

格蘭　　: 我不知道該說什麼。

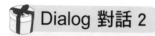 **Dialog 對話 2**

Grant is talking to Megan later that day.

之後，格蘭與梅格聊天。

G　　　: Megan, I'm desperate! I'm at the end of my tether! What can I do?

格蘭　　: 梅格，我感到絕望透頂了！我該怎麼辦？

M　　　: To win Helen back? Probably nothing...

梅格　　: 想挽回海倫嗎？也許沒有…。

G　　　: I can't believe I've lost her! We were together for three years. She's the love of my life!

格蘭　　: 我不相信自己已經失去她！我們已經在一起三年了！她是我一生所愛之人。

M　　　: Well, you may not like to hear this now, but soon the pain will pass.

梅格　　: 我現在說這句話也許讓你覺得不中聽，但是傷痛真的很快就會過去。

G　　　: No, no. It won't.

格蘭　　: 不會，不會，絕對不會的。

M　　　: Just give it time.

梅格　　: 時間會治療傷痛。

🎁 Dialog 對話 3

The next day, Grant calls Helen.

隔天，格蘭打電話給海倫。

G : Helen?

格蘭 : 海倫？

H : Yes. How are you, Grant?

海倫 : 我是。你好嗎，格蘭？

G : I'm...miserable.

格蘭 : 我…很痛苦。

H : Me, too. I made a mistake. I don't want us to be apart.

海倫 : 我也是。我犯了個錯誤，我不要我們分手。

G : Me, neither! I'm so sorry that I didn't pay enough attention to you.

格蘭 : 我也不要！很抱歉我對你不夠在乎。

H : And I'm sorry I ever listened to those silly rumors. I won't ever doubt you again.

海倫 : 我也很抱歉竟然聽信那些愚蠢的謠言。我不會再懷疑你了！

Useful Sentences 範例句型

Is it true what I heard?

我所聽聞的一切都是真的嗎？

Don't rush into a decision. Give it time.

不要妄下決定，多考慮一陣子。

Mandy couldn't believe that she'd lost her keys again.

曼蒂真不敢相信她又把鑰匙弄丟了！

Doug knew that his mother wouldn't like to hear it, but he had to tell her the bad news.

道格知道母親不想聽到這則壞消息，但是他還是必須告訴她。

Vocabulary 單字片語

☑ rumor	謠言
☑ swear	發誓
☑ break up	分手
☑ desperate	絕望的
☑ be at the end of one's tether	忍無可忍
☑ pain	痛苦
☑ apart	分手
☑ doubt	懷疑

That's What Friends Are For

朋友的意義

 Track-9

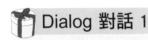 Dialog 對話 1

Megan calls her friend Paul on the phone.
梅格打電話給他的朋友保羅。

P : Hey, Meg! Long time no see!

保羅 : 嘿，梅格！好久不見！

M : Yes… I'm sorry, I meant to call you a couple of weeks ago, but I've been busy.

梅格 : 是啊！很抱歉，我本來在幾個禮拜之前就要打電話給你，但是我一直很忙。

P : That's OK. I understand. But you don't sound so good. Are you alright?

保羅 : 沒關係。我了解，但是你的聲音聽起來不太好。你還好吧？

M : No, not really. I'm really lonely here.

梅格 : 不好，很不好。我在這裡真的很孤單。

P : But haven't you made lots of new friends?

保羅 : 難道你沒有結交許多新朋友？

M　　 : Yes, but they're nothing like my old ones.

梅格　 : 有是有，但是他們一點也不像我的老朋友。

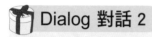 Dialog 對話 2

Paul and Megan continue their conversation.

保羅和梅格繼續他們的談話。

P　　 : 　When we talked last time, you seemed happy enough with your new friends.

保羅　 : 我們上次聊天時，你好像和新朋友相處得很愉快。

M　　 : I was. But now I've found out that lots of them gossip and spread rumors around. And I've also found that some people aren't reliable.

梅格　 : 我是啊！但是現在我發現，八卦及謠言滿天飛。而且我發現有些人不可靠。

P　　 : Well, people are people. And even in our circle of friends, nobody is perfect.

保羅　 : 有人就有人性。即使在我們的朋友圈，也沒有人是完美的。

M　　 : You always have such a positive way of looking at things! I guess you're right, though. Nobody is perfect. I wonder why that's getting me down now that I'm in Vancouver when I used to be able to accept it?

梅格　 : 你總是樂觀的看事情！你說得有道理，沒有人是完美

的。但我很納悶為什麼我以前可以接受，但是現在溫
哥華我卻悶悶不樂？

P   : You know what I think, Megan. You're just homesick.

保羅   : 你知道我的想法嗎？ 梅格，你只是想家吧！

M   : I think you're right.

梅格   : 我想你說得沒錯。

 Dialog 對話 3

Megan hears her roommate asking for the phone.

梅格聽到她的室友說要用電話。

M   : Sorry, I can't talk for much longer. But do you have any advice for me?

梅格   : 很抱歉。我不能再說了！你能提供我任何建議嗎？

P   : For curing homesickness?

保羅   : 治好我的思鄉病嗎？

M   : Yes, Dr Paul.

梅格   : 是的！保羅醫生。

P   : Well, there is a remedy; come home and visit!

保羅   : 有一帖藥方；就是回家探親。

M : That's a great idea, Paul. I think I'll try to get away for the weekend. I've got to go now, but thanks so much for listening to me.

梅格 : 這是個好主意，保羅。我想這個週末我會回家一趟。現在我得掛電話了，謝謝你聽我說心事。

P : Anytime, Meg. That's what friends are for!

保羅 : 梅格，隨時都可以和我談心。這就是朋友的意義啊！

Useful Sentences 範例句型

You seemed to enjoy yourself last week at the party!

上週末在宴會中，你好像很自得其樂。

She always has a positive way of looking at things.

他總是樂觀的看待事情。

Fiona went to the doctor, hoping he could cure her problem.

妃雅娜去看醫生，希望可以治癒她的毛病。

Gordon told his son that he couldn't watch TV for much longer.

葛登叫他兒子不准再看電視了。

Vocabulary 單字片語

☑ lonely　　　　　　　　　　　　　　孤獨的

☑ be nothing like …　　　　　　　　就只是像……

☑ spread something around　　　　四處流傳……

☑ reliable　　　　　　　　　　　　　可靠的

☑ get somebody down　　　　　　　讓某人心情低落

☑ homesick　　　　　　　　　　　　想家的

☑ accept　　　　　　　　　　　　　接受

☑ remedy　　　　　　　　　　　　　治療

MEMO

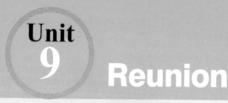
Reunion

重逢

Track-10

 Dialog 對話 1

Megan has decided to take Paul's advice and go home to visit for the weekend. As she has planned, she goes to meet Paul at a restaurant.

梅格已經決定採納保羅的建議，這個週末回家探親。她按照計劃和保羅在餐廳會面。

M   : Paul! It's so good to see you!

梅格 : 保羅！看見你真好！

P   : Me too! Have you lost weight?

保羅 : 我也是！你變瘦了嗎？

M   : Actually, yes! I've been going to the gym three times a week.

梅格 : 事實上，是的！我一星期上三次健身房。

P   : I didn't know that. I guess there's a lot that I've missed.

保羅 : 我不知道這件事。我想我錯過了許多關於你的事。

M   : Yep. But I plan on catching you up on everything.

梅格 : 是啊，但是我打算將所發生的事一五一十告訴你。

P　　　: Excellent! But first, let's order—I'm starving!

保羅　　: 很好！但是，先來點餐吧，我餓壞了！

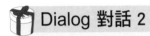 Dialog 對話 2

The waiter comes to take their orders. Megan goes first.

侍者前來寫菜單，梅格先點菜。

M　　　: I'd like to have a salad to start, please.

梅格　　: 請給我一份沙拉作為開胃菜。

P　　　: What kind of dressing would you like?

保羅　　: 你想要什麼醬料？

M　　　: Caesar. And for my main course, I'll have a hamburger.

梅格　　: 凱撒沙拉醬。至於主菜，我要一份漢堡。

P　　　: Anything to drink?

保羅　　: 想喝點什麼嗎？

M　　　: A diet coke, please.

梅格　　: 低糖的可樂。

P　　　: Coming right up!

保羅　　: 馬上來！

🎁 Dialog 對話 3

After their meal, Paul reaches for the bill.
點完餐後,保羅去拿帳單。

M   : No, Paul, let me pay.

梅格   : 不不,保羅,讓我來付。

P   : Really, I insist! It's my treat.

保羅   : 真的,我堅持要付!這頓我請。

M   : That's kind of you, thank you. Next time it's on me.

梅格   : 你真好!謝謝你。下一次換我請。

P   : Which reminds me, we should hang out more often. In fact, I'm thinking of coming to Vancouver next weekend.

保羅   : 你倒是提醒了我,我們應該經常相聚。事實上,我還在想下週去溫哥華。

M   : Really? That'd be cool! Do you need a place to stay?

梅格   : 真的嗎?那真是太好了!你需要找地方住嗎?

P   : No, I can stay with my cousin and now I know I can eat with you!

保羅   : 不用,我可以和我的表弟同住,但是吃飯時我就會找你!

Useful Sentences 範例句型

It's been a long time!

好久不見了！

It's been too long!

很久沒聯絡了！

What's new with you?

近來好吧？

Tell me all your news!

告訴我你所發生的一切！

Vocabulary 單字片語

☑ **weight**	重量
☑ **gym**	體育館
☑ **catch up**	趕上
☑ **starve**	飢餓
☑ **waiter**	侍者
☑ **salad**	沙拉
☑ **Caesar dressing**	凱撒沙拉醬
☑ **main course**	主餐
☑ **bill**	帳單
☑ **treat**	請客
☑ **it's on me**	我請客

Unit
10

Birds of a Feather
同好

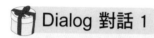 Dialog 對話 1

Celia and Kurt are chatting together during their lunch break.
莎莉亞和科特在午休時間一起聊天。

C : So have you heard the latest gossip?
梅格 : 你聽說了最新的八卦嗎？

K : No? What's the scoop?
科特 : 沒有？有什麼獨家新聞？

C : Megan has another boyfriend! His name is Paul and he's visiting from White Rock!
梅格 : 梅格另外也交了一位男朋友。他名叫保羅，從白石鎮來探訪他。

K : Really? Megan sure gets around.
科特 : 真的嗎？梅格一定跟他走得很近。

C : I know! Hey, there's Kim. I've got to run.
梅格 : 我知道！嘿！金來了！我得走了！

K : See you.
科特 : 再見。

🎁 Dialog 對話 2

Megan sees Kurt sitting alone.
梅格看見科特獨自一人坐著。

M : Hey Kurt, mind if I join you?
梅格 : 嘿！科特，可以坐你旁邊嗎？

K : Not at all. Hey, you just missed Celia. She just
left to see Kim.
科特 : 當然。你剛好錯過莎莉亞了，她才剛離開要見金。

M : Ah, Celia and Kim...they're birds of a feather.
梅格 : 噢！莎莉亞和金…她們都是那種人。

K : What do you mean by that?
科特 : 你這句話什麼意思？

M : Well, don't get me wrong. I like them both. It's
just that they both tend to say things that they
shouldn't. They like to gossip.
梅格 : 不要誤會，我不討厭她們兩個。只不過她們的閒言閒
語傳的太誇張，又喜歡說長道短。

K : Ah…
科特 : 啊…

M : Why are you turning red all of a sudden?
梅格 : 你為什麼突然這麼激動？

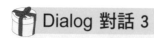 Dialog 對話 3

Kurt confesses that he's just heard some gossip about Megan from Celia.
科特坦承，他才剛從莎莉亞那裡聽到有關梅格的八卦。

M　　：What? She said what?
梅格　：什麼？她這麼說？

K　　：So it's not true?
科特　：所以，那不是真的囉！

M　　：Of course it's not true! Paul and I are just friends. What on earth made her think of such a thing?
梅格　：當然不是真的！保羅和我只是朋友。到底是什麼讓她聯想到那個地步？

K　　：I have no idea.
科特　：我不知道。

M　　：Would you do me a favor? Next time she starts gossiping, can you tell her to mind her own business? If she doesn't change her ways, then I'll find it impossible to be friends with her.
梅格　：你肯幫我一個忙嗎？下次她開始八卦時，你能不能請她不要多管閒事？如果她不收斂一下，我就不能再跟她做朋友了！

K　　：I can understand that. I'm sorry that I listened to her before.
科特　：我可以體諒，我很抱歉自己也曾把她的閒話聽進去。

Useful Sentences 範例句型

Marsha was so embarrassed that she turned red!

瑪莎糗的臉都紅了？

What on earth are you doing?

你到底做了什麼？

After Sam read her diary, Trudy told him to mind his own business.

山姆偷看褚蒂的日記，褚蒂不高興的要他管好自己就好。

Lily's study habits are bad. She should really try to change her ways.

麗莉的讀書習慣很差，她實在應該好好的改一改了。

Vocabulary 單字片語

☑ scoop	獨家新聞
☑ somebody gets around	和某人走得很近
☑ have to run	我得離開了
☑ birds of a feather	一丘之貉
☑ tend	傾向於…
☑ impossible	不可能

Chapter 2

Home Sweet Home!

甜蜜的家

Living in a dormitory can be exciting. It's a chance to meet other students, and have freedoms that one might not have while living with one's family. However, dorm life isn't always easy. Noisy or inconsiderate roommates can make things difficult, which is why so many students, when visiting their families, breathe a sigh of relief when the walk in their front doors thinking, "there's no place like home."

宿舍生活可能是有趣的。你可以認識其他學生，擁有寄宿在別人家裡所沒有的自由。然而，宿舍生活也不是這麼簡單，吵雜聲或是不夠善解人意的室友會讓人一肚子怨氣。這就是為什麼會有這麼多的學生在返家探親時，一步入大門時，就會喘一口大氣感嘆：「還是自己的家最好！」

Unit 1

Where Do You Live?

你家住哪裡？

 Dialog 對話 1

Megan is talking to Kurt after intramurals.
參加完校內運動社後，梅格和科特交談。

M : So, do you live in one of the dorms?
梅格 : 那麼，你就住在這宿舍裡？

K : I do. It's too far for me to commute here from my parents' home.
科特 : 對啊！從我父母家到這裡通勤太遠了！

M : Where do they live?
梅格 : 他們住在哪裡呀？

K : In Smithers! It takes about ten hours to drive there from here. How about yours?
科特 : 住在史密澤市！從那裡開車到這裡約需十個小時。你們家住哪裡？

M : My family lives in White Rock. Do you like dorm life?
梅格 : 我家住在白石鎮。你喜歡宿舍生活嗎？

K   : I do … except that I miss my mother's cooking!

科特   : 我喜歡…，但是我很懷念媽媽煮的菜。

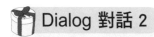 Dialog 對話 2

Later, Megan is talking to Grant.

稍後，梅格與格蘭交談。

G   : We should invite Kurt and Celia to come with us to the movies this weekend.

格蘭   : 我們應該邀請科特和莎莉亞這禮拜六和我們一起去看電影。

M   : That's a good idea—except I know that Kurt won't be able to make it.

梅格   : 好主意。不過我知道科特不會來的。

G   : Really? Why not?

格蘭   : 真的嗎？為什麼不會？

M   : He's going to Smithers.

梅格   : 他要去史密澤市。

G   : Smithers? Why on earth is he going there?

格蘭   : 史密澤市？他幹嘛要去那裡？

M   : That's where he's from! He's going to visit his family.

梅格   : 那是他的故鄉！他要返鄉探親。

🎁 Dialog 對話 3

Grant calls Celia to invite her to the movies with him and Megan.
格蘭打電話給莎莉亞邀請她和梅格一起看電影。

G : So, you'll come then?

格蘭 : 那你會來嗎？

C : I'd love to. It's too bad Kurt can't make it, though.

莎莉亞 : 我當然來。科特不能來，真是太可惜了！

G : Yes, but he hasn't visited his family in over a month.

格蘭 : 是啊！但是他已經一個多月沒有回家看自己的家人了！

C : I can understand that. I feel pretty lucky that my parents live close enough to school that I can still live with them.

莎莉亞 : 我可以體會這種事。我覺得自己很幸運，父母家和學校住得這麼近，所以我現在仍然可以和父母同住。

G : You are lucky! You don't have to pay rent like the rest of us.

格蘭 : 你很幸運！你不必像我們其他人還得付房租。

C : And, I never get homesick!

莎莉亞 : 而且，我也絕對不會得到思鄉病。

Useful Sentences 範例句型

How far away is it?

有多遠？

It's been over a year since I've seen her.

我已經一年沒見過她了！

She's about 160cm tall.

她大約 160 公分高。

George wants to come, but he can't though

喬治想來，但是卻不能來。

Vocabulary 單字片語

☑ commute		通勤
☑ except		除了…之外
☑ invite		邀請
☑ make it		成功；達到目標
☑ on earth		究竟；到底
☑ rent		出租
☑ homesick		想家的

Unit 2

How Many People Are There in Your Family?

你家有幾個人？

 Track-13

 Dialog 對話 1

Kurt has just returned from Smithers. He and Megan are having coffee at the student union building.

科特剛從史密澤市回來。他和梅格在學生活動中心喝咖啡。

M   : How was your trip?

梅格   : 你的史密澤之旅怎樣啊？

K   : It was great! We had a big family dinner on Saturday night. All my brothers were there, and so were a few of my cousins.

科特   : 很棒！我們禮拜六晚上全家吃大餐。我的哥哥弟弟都在，一些表兄弟也都在。

M   : That sounds nice. Do you have a big family?

梅格   : 聽起來很不錯。你們是大家庭嗎？

K   : Yes. I have three older brothers, and two youngers.

科特   : 沒錯。我有三個哥哥，兩個弟弟。

64

M   : That's a lot of boys! How many aunts and uncles do you have?

梅格   : 男生很多。你有幾個姑嬸和叔伯啊？

K   : Let's see…my mother is an only child, but my father has two sisters and a brother, and each of them is married. So that makes three aunts, and three uncles!

科特   : 我想想…我媽媽是獨生女，但是我爸爸有兩個姊妹和一個哥哥。他們都已經結婚了。所以我有三位姑嬸及兩位叔伯。

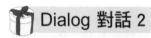 Dialog 對話 2

Kurt and Megan continue their discussion.
科特和梅格繼續他們的討論。

K   : So, what about you? How many people are there in your family?

科特   : 那你呢？你們家有幾個人？

M   : Just four; my mother, father, sister, and me.

梅格   : 四個；我媽、我爸、我姊妹、和我。

K   : Is your sister older or younger than you?

科特   : 是姊姊還是妹妹？

M   : She's four years older than me.

梅格   : 是比我大四歲的姊姊。

K   : Are you close?

科特 : 你們感情很好嗎？

M   : Well, we used to fight all the time when we were kids. But now we get along pretty well.

梅格 : 我們小時後常常吵吵鬧鬧，但是現在我們處得很好。

K   : Do you see her often?

科特 : 你常去看她嗎？

M   : Unfortunately not. I'm here in Vancouver studying—and she's doing a master's degree in England!

梅格 : 很遺憾的，並沒有。我在溫哥華這裡唸書，她則在英國攻讀碩士。

 Dialog 對話 3

Kurt asks Megan if she has any grandparents.
科特問梅格有沒有爺爺奶奶。

M   : Yes. My mother's parents are still alive. They live with my uncle and his family.

梅格 : 有，我外公外婆還健在。他們住我舅舅那。

K   : In White Rock?

科特 : 住在白石鎮嗎？

M   : Yes. Actually, they live in the same apartment building as my parents!

梅格　：對。事實上，他們和我的父母住在同一棟公寓裡。

K　　：That's nice that you're all so close! I've never met my grandparents.

科特　：你們大家都這麼親密是一件好事。我從未見過我的爺爺奶奶。

M　　：Why not?

梅格　：為什麼？

K　　：My mother's parents died before I was born; my father's parents live in mainland China, and I haven't had a chance to travel there yet.

科特　：外公外婆在我出生之前就已經去世了！我爺爺奶奶則是住在中國大陸；我一直都沒有機會去那裡。

Useful Sentences 範例句型

Mario and his brother are very close.

　　馬利歐和他的兄弟非常親密。

Susan failed the test because she didn't have a chance to study.

　　蘇珊沒時間唸書，所以她考試不及格。

Do you go to the movies often?

　　你常去看電影嗎？

I used to like playing video games, but I don't anymore.

我以前喜歡打電玩，但我現在不喜歡了！

Vocabulary 單字片語

☑ return from		從…返回
☑ a few		一些
☑ sounds nice		聽起來不錯
☑ older		較年長的
☑ younger		較年輕的
☑ aunt		嬸嬸（姑姑、阿姨、舅母）
☑ uncle		叔伯
☑ married		已婚的
☑ get along		相處

MEMO

....

....

....

....

....

....

Dorm Life
宿舍生活

 Dialog 對話 1

Megan is visiting Grant is his dorm room.
梅格到格蘭的宿舍房間找他。

G : I'm getting a little sick of living in the dorm.
格蘭 : 我已經對宿舍生活感到厭煩了！

M : Really? Why is that?
梅格 : 真的嗎？為什麼會這樣？

G : It's too crowded and too noisy.
格蘭 : 宿舍太擁擠且太吵雜了！

M : Well, it's not luxury accommodation! But at least it's cheap.
梅格 : 這個嘛，沒有高級享受，但至少價錢便宜。

G : I guess so, but I still wish there was more space in this room and that I had more privacy.
格蘭 : 我想也是。但是我仍然希望能有更大的空間；及較多的隱私。

M : You get what you pay for!
梅格 : 一分錢一分貨！

🎁 Dialog 對話 2

Grant has gone to the bathroom, and Megan has stayed in his room. There's a knock on the door.

格蘭去浴室，梅格則待在格蘭的房間裡。此時，有人敲門。

M　　：Come in!

梅格　：請進！

N　　：Oh, hi! My name is Neil. I'm Grant's neighbor. Is he around?

尼爾　：噢！嗨！我叫做尼爾。我是格蘭的鄰居。他在嗎？

M　　：No, he just went to the bathroom, but he'll be back soon.

梅格　：不在，他剛去浴室，但是馬上就會回來了！

N　　：Actually, I don't have time to wait. I need a clean shirt to wear on my date tonight.

尼爾　：事實上，我沒有時間等，我需要換一件乾淨的襯衫晚上約會穿。

M　　：And you want to borrow one of Grant's?

梅格　：你想要借格蘭的襯衫穿？

N　　：I'm sure he won't mind! Ah, this blue one is nice—and it's still got the tags on it! Thanks! Bye!

尼爾　：我相信他不會介意！噢！這件藍色的襯衫不錯—價格牌還在上面咧！謝啦！再見！

Dialog 對話 3

Grant has just returned from the bathroom and Megan tells him about meeting his neighbor.

格蘭剛從浴室回來，梅格見過他的鄰居的事告訴格蘭。

G : What?! That guy is known for borrowing stuff without asking. And for not returning it!

格蘭 : 什麼？這傢伙素來就惡名昭彰，老是沒開口問就向人借東西，而且還借了不還。

M : I'm sorry! If I'd known, I wouldn't have let him take your shirt. I just assumed that he was your friend.

梅格 : 抱歉！我如果早知道這樣，就不會讓他拿走你的襯衫了！我還以為他是你的朋友。

G : Never mind. But this is exactly what I don't like about living with so many people.

格蘭 : 算了啦，這就是為什麼我不喜歡和這麼多人同住的原因了！

M : Don't they respect you or your things?

梅格 : 他們難道不尊重你或是尊重你的物品嗎？

G : No, and they make a big mess in the bathroom! You should have seen what it was like a minute ago! The toilet was overflowing and...

格蘭 : 不會，他們總是把浴室弄得亂七八糟！你應該來看看一分鐘前浴室的慘狀！整個浴室淹滿了水，還有…

71

M : You've said enough! It sounds like it's time for you to move out of the dorm and into your own apartment!

梅格 : 夠了夠了！看來的確是你該搬出來住的時候了！

Useful Sentences 範例句型

When the used car I bought broke down, my mother told me that I got what I paid for.

我買的二手車拋錨時，我的母親告誡我一分錢一分貨的道理。

Who's that knocking at the door?

誰在敲門？

There was no space on the bus for any more people.

公車已經客滿了！

Excuse me, I'm looking for Samantha. Is she around?

很抱歉！我要找莎曼珊。她有在這嗎？

It's time that you started studying more.

該是你更用功的時候了！

Vocabulary 單字片語

☑ be sick of somebody/something	厭煩某人 / 某事
☑ crowded	擁擠的
☑ noisy	吵雜的
☑ luxury	奢侈的
☑ accommodation	膳宿
☑ cheap	便宜的
☑ privacy	隱私
☑ assume	假設
☑ toilet	廁所
☑ overflow	溢出來

MEMO

Unit 4

Renting an Apartment
租公寓

 Dialog 對話 1

Megan is helping Grant to make a list with the things he wants in his new apartment.
梅格正在幫格蘭歸納整理他心目中的理想公寓條件。

M : So, what kind of place do you want to live in?
梅格 : 那麼，你想要住哪一種房子？

G : Well, I don't want anything too small. At least three times as big as the dorm room.
格蘭 : 我不想要住在太小的地方，至少要比宿舍大三倍才行。

M : That's pretty big for one guy! Do you want a one bedroom, or a studio?
梅格 : 你一個人要住這麼大間！要隔間還是沒隔間？

G : Either is fine, I'm not picky. Just as long as it has twenty-four hour security, a nice patio, and hardwood floors.
格蘭 : 都可以，我不挑。只要有二十四小時的警衛、一處不錯的內院及原木地板。

M : And what about the location?
梅格 : 地點呢？

G : On the West Side. Somewhere close to school so that I don't have to spend a lot of time commuting.

格蘭 : 西區，接近學校的地方，這樣我就不必花很多時間往返。

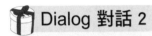 Dialog 對話 2

Megan asks Grant if he has any other requirements for an apartment.

梅格詢問格蘭對於公寓是否還有其他的要求。

G : Come to think of it, just one other thing. I'd like to have a view of the mountains.

格蘭 : 仔細想想，另外還有一個條件，我想要可以眺望山景的視野。

M : You are a discerning customer! And what, may I ask, is your budget?

梅格 : 你這客戶要求也太多了吧！可否容我問一下，你的預算是多少？

G : Well, I pay 250 every month to live in the dorm. But I realize that I'll have to spend a little more to get what I want.

格蘭 : 我的宿舍費是每個月二百五十。那麼要住我心目中的理想房間，勢必得多花一點錢。

M : A little more? Are you dreaming? Apartments like the one you described cost an arm and a leg.

梅格 : 多花「一點」錢？你在作什麼夢？符合你要求的公寓可是要花一大筆錢的。

G : Are you sure? Maybe if we check the classifieds, we'll find the apartment of my dreams.

格蘭 : 真的嗎？説不定翻翻分類廣告，就可以找到我心目中房子了。

M : Maybe we should just check your head!

梅格 : 應該先翻翻你的腦袋是不是有問題！

 Dialog 對話 3

Grant opens his newspaper to the classifieds section.

格蘭翻開報紙的分類廣告欄。

M : It doesn't look like there are many mansions going cheaply this week!

梅格 : 這禮拜好像有滿多的廉租公寓！

G : Very funny. What about this one: "3-bedroom, en suite, laundry, parking, gym in building. Call Tony."

格蘭 : 有趣。這個如何：「三房；套房；附洗衣室、車位、健身房。請電洽東尼。」

M : But the price isn't listed. Maybe this one:"One bedroom, air conditioned, furnished. Shared bathroom. 300 a month."

梅格 : 但是並沒有寫房租。這個應該不錯：「一房；附空調、家具；公共浴室。月租三百。」

G : No shared bathrooms. What else is there in here?

格蘭 : 不考慮公共衛浴。還有其他的嗎？

M : Not much else. Maybe you should just face it. You're stuck with the dorm!

梅格 : 不多了！也許你應該認命，好好窩在宿舍裡！

G : I don't give up so easily! My sister's friend is a real estate agent. I'll just give her a call!

格蘭 : 我不會這麼輕易就放棄的！我妹妹的朋友是不動產仲介。我要打個電話給她！

Useful Sentences 範例句型

That's going to cost an arm and a leg!

那可是一筆天文數字！

When Tom asked Jill to marry him, she told him that he must be dreaming!

當湯姆跟姬兒求婚時，她回說他一定是在做白日夢！

Keep trying! Don't give up so easily!

加油！不要輕易放棄！

If you need any help, just give me a call.

如果你需要任何的協助，儘管撥電話給我。

Mandy's parents went out so she was stuck looking after her little sister.

曼蒂的父母外出，所以她被困在家裡照顧小妹妹。

Lucas had to face it: there was no way he could pass the test.

盧卡斯只得認命，因為他根本不可能通過考試。

Vocabulary 單字片語

☑	list	清單
☑	studio	起居室與臥室合一的房間
☑	picky	挑剔的
☑	security	安全
☑	patio	內院；天井
☑	hardwood floor	硬木地版
☑	location	地點
☑	requirement	條件；要求
☑	view	視野景觀
☑	discerning	敏銳的；有識別力的
☑	budget	預算
☑	realize	了解
☑	en suite	套房
☑	laundry	洗衣間
☑	parking	停車

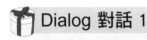
Dialog 對話 1

Grant is meeting Lena, a real estate agent, to look at a few apartments.

格蘭與不動產仲介蓮娜見面，他們要去看新公寓。

L : I've lined up three apartments for us to look at this afternoon.

蓮娜 : 我已經安排了三間公寓，準備今天下午去看一看。

G : I can't wait to see them.

格蘭 : 我等不及要去看了！

L : I have to be honest with you. It wasn't possible to find any place that was as nice as you wanted for so small a budget.

蓮娜 : 我必須老實告訴你，由於你的預算實在不多，因此要找到符合你要求的房子，根本不可能。

G : That's OK. I realize now that my expectations might have been too high.

格蘭 : 沒關係。我現在知道我的期望過高了。

L : Nevertheless, I was pleasantly surprised by what is on the market right now.

蓮娜 : 不過，我還是很高興的告訴你，現在還有很多不錯的房子可供選擇。

G : Really? You're raising my hopes! You'd better say no more and let the apartments speak for themselves!

格蘭 : 真的？你增加了我的希望！你先不用多說，讓房子自己來說話吧！

🎁 Dialog 對話 2

Grant and Lena have just finished looking at an apartment on the fifth floor of a building.
格蘭和蓮娜剛看完一棟六樓的公寓。

G : Well, it doesn't have much of a view…but it is nice and clean.

格蘭 : 沒什麼景觀…但是很精緻、乾淨。

L : And in a great location! It's close to public transportation.

蓮娜 : 而且地點很好！接近大眾運輸系統。

G : It's not huge, though.

格蘭 : 可是不大。

L	: But big enough for one person. And it's got big closets for storage.
蓮娜	: 一個人住就夠大了！而且還有大儲藏櫃。

G	: …and a full kitchen so that I can cook my own meals.
格蘭	: …還有完善的廚房，我可以自己開伙。

L	: You'll save a lot of money if you cook for yourself. But the rent isn't too bad.
蓮娜	: 你若自己開伙，就可以省下許多錢。而且租金也不會很貴。

G	: You're right. This apartment is a good value. I'll take it!
格蘭	: 你說的對。這間公寓很值得，我租了！

 Dialog 對話 3

Grant and Lena are in Lena's office.
格蘭和蓮娜在她的辦公室裡。

L	: So, you'll have to sign a lease if you want to rent the apartment. The landlord wants a tenant who can stay for at least a year.
蓮娜	: 如果你要租房子，你就得簽租約。房東都希望房客可以住滿一年。

G　　　: No problem. I won't be done with school for at least three more years!

格蘭　: 沒問題。我至少要三年後才會畢業！

L　　　: And you'll have to pay a deposit to cover any damage you may do to the apartment.

蓮娜　: 還得付押金，以便抵繳公寓損壞的費用。

G　　　: Sure. Will you accept a check?

格蘭　: 當然。你收支票嗎？

L　　　: Yes. I'll also need post-dated checks for rent covering your tenancy. You can make the checks out to the landlord, Mr. Lin.

蓮娜　: 收。我也希望你開好租期之內的所有期票。支票的抬頭是房東林先生。

G　　　: Alright. So, when can I move in?

格蘭　: 好。那麼我什麼時候可以搬進去？

L　　　: As soon as you like. But there's just one more thing.

蓮娜　: 隨時都可以。還有一件事。

G　　　: What's that?

格蘭　: 什麼事？

L　　　: My fee. I get half of one month's rent!

蓮娜　: 仲介費。我的佣金是房租的一半！

Useful Sentences 範例句型

Bobby couldn't wait for the baseball game to start.

巴比等不及要看棒球賽開始。

It's always better to be honest with someone than to tell a lie.

誠實待人總比對人說謊來得好！

The salesman stopped talking and let the car speak for itself.

推銷員不再推銷下去，而讓車子本身來證明。

Mark will go to university as soon as he's finished high school.

馬可完成高中學業後，就要馬上升大學。

Vocabulary 單字片語

☑ line something up	排成一行；就位
☑ expectations	期望
☑ pleasantly	愉悅地
☑ market	市場
☑ raise	提高
☑ floor	樓層；地板
☑ huge	大的

☑	transportation	交通
☑	closets	櫃子
☑	storage	儲存
☑	value	價值
☑	lease	租賃
☑	landlord	房東
☑	tenant	租戶
☑	damage	損毀
☑	check	支票
☑	accept	接受
☑	fee	費用

MEMO

....

....

....

....

....

....

....

....

Unit
6 Moving
搬家

Track-17

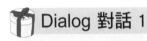 Dialog 對話 1

Megan is talking to Josh, Grant's roommate in the dorm.
梅格正在和格蘭住宿舍時的室友賈許交談。

M : So, you're going to miss Grant?
梅格 : 這樣一來，你會想念格蘭嗎？

J : No way! Now I get this room all to myself! Plus, I can visit Grant over at his place any time. Think of all the great parties we'll have!
賈許 : 一點也不！現在這間房間就完全屬於我的了！而且我隨時都可以到格蘭住的地方去找他。我們以後就可以開很多派對了！

M : But first we have to move Grant's stuff.
梅格 : 但是首先我們得將格蘭的東西搬走。

J : Thankfully, he doesn't have much, just these few boxes.
賈許 : 好在他的東西不多，就只有這幾箱而已！

M : That's it? I guess Grant's lucky that his new place is furnished.

梅格 : 就只有這些嗎？格蘭很幸運，他的新家有附家具。

J : And so are we—we don't have to break our backs helping him move beds and sofas!

賈許 : 我們也很幸運，因為這樣我們就不必冒著折斷背脊的危險，幫他搬床及沙發！

 Dialog 對話 2

Megan and Josh are loading boxes into the trunk of a car.
梅格和賈許正將箱子裝進車子的後行李箱內。

J : Grant's lucky his parents were willing to lend him their car to move his stuff!

賈許 : 格蘭很幸運，他的父母願意把車子借給他搬家。

M : I'll say. It's not cheap to hire movers. Besides, with as little stuff as Grant has, it wouldn't have been worth it.

梅格 : 沒錯，請搬家工人可不便宜。再說，格蘭的東西這麼少，雇搬家工人並不划算。

J : Especially since he has our help for free!

賈許 : 尤其是還有我們免費幫他忙咧！

M : Speaking of help, where is Grant? I've started to feel like we're doing all the work.

梅格 : 說到幫忙，格蘭在哪裡？我已經想動工了！

J	:	Don't worry...he'll do his fair share once you get to his new place.
賈許	:	別擔心，一旦到了他的新家，就是他該自己動手的時候了。

M	:	Only because he'll have too. There's only enough room in the car for one passenger, so he'll have to pitch in more.
梅格	:	看來他也必須如此。因為車子的空間僅能容納一位乘客，沒有幫手他當然只能自己加油！

 ## Dialog 對話 2

Megan and Grant are at Grant's new building. Megan is holding the elevator while Grant pushes boxes into it.

梅格和格蘭已經到了新公寓，梅格幫格蘭把電梯按住，好讓他把箱子家當推進電梯。

G	:	Just one more!
格蘭	:	只要再一趟就好了！

M	:	Finished?
梅格	:	都搬完了嗎？

G	:	Yep, all done. Man, this has been hard work!
格蘭	:	對，全都好了。老天，真是苦差事！

M	:	Tell me about it. Now, what floor are you on?
梅格	:	現在請告訴我。你要去幾樓？

G	: The fifth!
格蘭	: 六樓！

M	: New apartment, here we come!
梅格	: 新家，我們來了！

Useful Sentences 範例句型

Kim was over at Lyle's house studying.

> 金到麗莉家唸書。

Morris has been feeling better, especially since he exercises every day.

> 莫理斯覺得舒服多了，尤其是他每天做完運動後。

Speaking of water, I need to buy some at the store.

> 說到水，我得去店裡買一些。

Judith had her fair share of homework to do every night.

> 茱蒂絲每天晚上都有份內的作業待完成。

Vocabulary 單字片語

☑ room	房間
☑ place	地方

☑	stuff	物品；東西
☑	boxes	箱子
☑	furnished	附家具的
☑	thankfully	感謝地；好在
☑	break one's back	折斷背脊
☑	sofa	沙發
☑	truck	後行李箱
☑	load	裝載
☑	hire	雇用
☑	pitch in	打起精神
☑	passenger	乘客
☑	elevator	電梯

MEMO

....

....

....

....

....

....

....

Dialog 對話 1

Grant has settled into his new apartment. The phone rings and Grant answers—it's his girlfriend from White Rock, Helen.

格蘭已經在新公寓落腳了！電話響了，格蘭接聽。是他在白石鎮的女友，海倫打來的。

G　　：Hello?

格蘭　：哈囉？

H　　：Grant? It's Helen.

海倫　：格蘭？我是海倫。

G　　：Helen! I can hardly recognize your voice! Are you OK?

格蘭　：海倫！我幾乎聽不出來你的聲音！你還好吧？

H　　：Actually, no. I'm really sick.

海倫　：事實上不好，我生重病了。

G　　：Will you be able to make it to my housewarming party tonight?

格蘭　：你能不能撐著來參加我今晚的新居派對？

H : Unfortunately, no. But don't worry about me. You have a good time with your friends. I'll come over and see your place next weekend.

海倫 : 很遺憾，恐怕不行。但是別擔心我，你可以和好朋友盡情玩樂。下週末我會來參觀你住的地方。

 Dialog 對話 2

Grant's first guests have arrived. He is chatting with them when the buzzer on the intercom rings.

格蘭的第一批客人已經到來。對講機響時，他正在和他們聊天。

G : Excuse me—there's someone downstairs! Hello?
格蘭 : 對不起，有人按對講機！哈囉？

M : Hey, Grant! It's Megan! Can you ring me up?
梅格 : 嘿！格蘭！是我梅格！你可以開門讓我上樓嗎？

G : Yep, just a second.
格蘭 : 好，稍等一下。

M : And I've forgotten : what's your apartment number again?
梅格 : 還有，我忘記你家幾號了，可以再跟我講一次嗎？

G : Number 12, fifth floor, remember?
格蘭 : 十二號六樓，記住了嗎？

M　　　: Got it! See you soon.

梅格　　: 知道了！再見。

 Dialog 對話 3

Grant's party is over. He is saying goodbye to the last of his guests.

格蘭的宴會已結束。他正在和他的最後一位客人道別。

G　　　: Thank you so much for coming.

格蘭　　: 真的很感謝你能來。

C　　　: Thanks so much for inviting me!

客人　　: 我也很感謝你邀請我來！

G　　　: Do you need a ride home? I can call a taxi for you.

格蘭　　: 你要搭車回家嗎？我可以替你叫計程車。

C　　　: Thanks, but that's OK. My sister will be here in a minute to pick me up and take me home.

客人　　: 謝了，不用了。我姊等一下就會來接我回家。

G　　　: Oh, here's the elevator.

格蘭　　: 噢！電梯來了！

C　　　: Thanks again for having me. I'll see you in class on Monday!

客人　　: 再謝謝你一次，星期一上課見！

Useful Sentences 範例句型

The teacher told us to wait a second before we started the test.

老師要我們等一下再開始考試。

Ingrid could hardly believe what she was seeing.

英葛瑞簡直無法相信自己眼見的。

The last of the students got off the bus at Main Street.

最後一個學生在主幹道下了車。

Henry rode his motorcycle to the store to pick up his sister.

亨利騎摩托車去店裡接他妹。

Vocabulary 單字片語

☑ **housewarming** 新居派對；喬遷慶宴

☑ **settle** 安定；定居

☑ **ring** 鈴響

☑ **recognize** 認出

☑ **voice** 聲音

☑ **buzzer** 信號器

☑ **intercom** 對講機

☑ **downstairs** 樓下

Unit 8

What's Cooking?

在煮什麼？

Track-19

 Dialog 對話 1

Grant is expecting his girlfriend, Helen, to come over to his new place. There's a knock at the door.

格蘭正期待海倫的來到時，敲門聲響起。

| G | : Helen! You're early! |
| 格蘭 | : 海倫！你早到了！ |

| H | : I know. I couldn't wait to see you! |
| 海倫 | : 我知道。我等不及要見你！ |

| G | : I'm glad you're here! Come in, come in. Let me take your coat. |
| 格蘭 | : 很高興你來這兒！請進！請進！我替你拿外套。 |

| H | : Thank you. My, this certainly is nicer than the dorm. |
| 海倫 | : 謝謝你。老天，這裡真的比宿舍好呢。 |

| G | : Thanks! I'm enjoying all the space. I have a balcony, my own bathroom, and a kitchen. |
| 格蘭 | : 謝啦！我喜歡這裡的每個地方，我有陽台、自己的浴室、及廚房。 |

H   : That explains why it smells so good in here! You must be cooking!

海倫   : 這就是為什麼這裡會有這麼香的味道吧！你一定是在煮飯！

 Dialog 對話 2

Grant and Helen go into the kitchen.
格蘭和海倫走進廚房。

H   : What are you making?
海倫   : 你在煮什麼？

G   : Spaghetti and tomato sauce...your favorite!
格蘭   : 義大利麵和番茄醬料…你的最愛！

H   : How thoughtful! I never knew you could cook!
海倫   : 太體貼了！我都不知道你還會煮飯！

G   : Neither did I! Actually, this is an experiment. It's the first time I've used my kitchen.
格蘭   : 我也不知道！事實上，我只是先實驗練習，順便使用一下新廚房。

H   : Ah, so I'm your guinea pig then! Do you need a hand with anything?
海倫   : 噢，原來我是白老鼠！需要我幫忙嗎？

G : Nope, I've got everything under control. The sauce will be ready in about fifteen minutes. In the meantime, I can give you a tour of the apartment.

格蘭 : 不用，一切都在我的掌握之中。醬料約十五分鐘就會弄好。在這段空檔，我可以帶你參觀公寓。

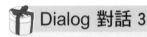 Dialog 對話 3

Ten minutes later, Helen interrupts Grant.
十分鐘後，海倫打斷了格蘭。

H : What's that?
海倫 : 那是什麼？

G : What's what?
格蘭 : 什麼是什麼？

H : That smell! I think something is burning…
海倫 : 那個味道啊！我想可能有東西燒焦了….。

G : The sauce!
格蘭 : 醬料！

Grant runs to the kitchen)
（格蘭跑進廚房）

Oh no! It's ruined. I left the heat on too high and the sauce has burned.

噢，不！毀了！我把溫度調太高了！醬料全焦了！

| H | : | That's too bad. Luckily, I see you have the most important thing any bachelor could have in his kitchen. |
| 海倫 | : | 真糟糕。幸運的是，單身漢的廚房裡最重要的東西，你也具備喔。 |

| G | : | What? A fire extinguisher? |
| 格蘭 | : | 是什麼？滅火器嗎？ |

| H | : | No. The Yellow Pages! Flip to "pizza" and we'll order some take-out! |
| 海倫 | : | 不是，是電話簿！請翻到「披薩」的頁碼，然後叫個外送吧。 |

Useful Sentences 範例句型

It is rude to interrupt others when they are speaking.

打斷別人講話，很沒禮貌。

Kim forgot to study for the test, but luckily she still passed.

雖然金忘記唸書，她還是幸運地過關。

Jim didn't look nervous because he had everything under control.

吉姆因為事事都在他的掌握之中，所以一點也不緊張。

This is the first time I've traveled to America.

這是我第一次到美國旅行。

Vocabulary 單字片語

☑	expect	期望
☑	early	早的
☑	coat	外套
☑	certainly	當然
☑	balcony	陽台
☑	explain	解釋
☑	spaghetti	義大利麵
☑	sauce	醬料
☑	guinea pig	白老鼠
☑	need a hand	需要幫忙
☑	in the meantime	在這同時
☑	tour	旅行
☑	interrupt	打斷
☑	burn	燃燒
☑	ruin	毀壞
☑	bachelor	單身漢
☑	fire extinguisher	滅火器
☑	take-out	外帶

Unit 9

Honey, I'm Home!

親愛的，我回來了！

Track-20

 Dialog 對話 1

Grant is in White Rock, visiting his parents on the weekend.

週末，格蘭到白石鎮探訪父母。

G : Hey, mom! Long time, no see!

格蘭 : 嗨！媽！好久不見！

M : Grant! You're so thin!

媽 : 格蘭！你怎麼瘦成這樣！

G : I know! I haven't been eating well since I left the dorm. I don't like my own cooking.

格蘭 : 我知道！自從我搬離宿舍後，就沒有好好吃過東西。我不喜歡自己煮的菜。

M : I'll have to fatten you up while you're home this weekend!

媽 : 我得趁你這個週末在家的時候好好把你養胖。

G : Fine by me! And, if you don't mind, I'd like to lend a hand in the kitchen. Maybe I'll pick up a few things.

格蘭 : 求之不得！如果你不介意，我想要到廚房幫忙，也許我可以偷學一點技術。

M   : Like my secret recipe for spaghetti!

媽   : 好比說我的義大利麵食譜！

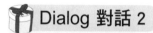 **Dialog 對話 2**

Grant's father walks in the front door.

格蘭的父親進了家門。

F   : Honey, I'm home!

爸   : 親愛的，我回家了！

M   : Hello, dear! How was work?

媽   : 哈囉！親愛的！上班還好吧？

F   : Fine. Is Grant here yet?

爸   : 很好。格蘭在嗎？

M   : He is. And never guess what your son is up to right now.

媽   : 他在！你絕對猜不到現在你的兒子在做什麼。

F   : I'm all ears.

爸   : 我洗耳恭聽。

M   : He's in the kitchen helping to prepare dinner!

媽   : 他正在廚房準備晚餐！

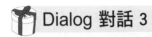 Dialog 對話 3

Grant is sitting down to dinner with his family. His sister, Jenny, helps herself to more fried rice.

格蘭和他的家人坐下來吃晚餐。他的姊姊珍妮又再盛了一些炒飯。

G : Hey, save some for the rest of us!

格蘭 : 嘿!留一點給我們其他人!

J : Sorry! But this rice is great! Mom, you've outdone yourself, again!

珍妮 : 不好意思!只是這飯太好吃了!媽,你又再次超越了自己的技藝!

G : For your information, dear sister, I made the rice!

格蘭 : 答案僅供參考,親愛的姊姊,飯是我做的!

J : You did not! You couldn't cook to save your life!

珍妮 : 才不是咧!你根本不會煮飯填飽自己的肚子!

G : Not only did I make the rice, but I steamed the vegetables and helped with the fish!

格蘭 : 我不但炒了這個飯,還燙了蔬菜。煮魚我也有幫忙呢!

J : Wow! Maybe you're in the wrong field at school! Instead of studying history, maybe you should go into the culinary arts!

珍妮 : 哇!也許你在學校唸錯學科了!你不應該去念歷史,而該去念烹飪!

G　　: I'll take that as a compliment. But really all the credit goes to my teacher—mom!

格蘭　: 我就把這個當作是讚美了。不過説真的，這些都是我的好師父，媽媽教導有方！

Useful Sentences 範例句型

Larry said it was fine by him if Julia wanted to make dinner.

賴瑞説，假如茱莉亞想準備晚餐，他會很高興。

Do you know Polly's secret recipe for cookies?

你知道寶莉的秘密烹飪食譜嗎？

You'll never guess what I got you for your birthday!

你絕對猜不到我為你準備什麼生日禮物！

The phone rang just as we were sitting down to dinner.

我們坐下來吃晚餐時，電話正好響起。

Vocabulary 單字片語

☑ honey	親愛的
☑ thin	瘦的
☑ fatten	使變胖
☑ recipe	食譜

☑ be up to something　　　　　　　做；從事

☑ be all ears　　　　　　　　　　　洗耳恭聽

☑ prepare　　　　　　　　　　　　準備

☑ outdo oneself　　　　　　　　　超越了自己

☑ steam　　　　　　　　　　　　　蒸

☑ culinary arts　　　　　　　　　烹飪

☑ credit　　　　　　　　　　　　　功績

☑ compliment　　　　　　　　　　讚美

MEMO

Unit 10

Home Alone
獨自在家

Track-21

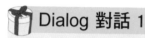 Dialog 對話 1

It's Sunday and Grant is getting ready to leave his parents' home and go back to Vancouver.

今天是星期天，格蘭正準備離開爸媽家，回溫哥華去。

M : The weekend has gone by too fast! It seems like you just got here.

媽 : 週末的日子過得太快了！感覺你好像才剛回到這兒似的。

G : I know. I'll miss you guys when I'm all alone back in my apartment.

格蘭 : 我知道。我一人回到孤孤單單的公寓時，一定會想念你們的。

M : I worry about you being there all alone. I wish you had stayed at the dorm.

媽 : 我很擔心你一個人在那裡孤單寂寞。我希望你能住在宿舍裡。

G : Well, to be honest, it can be a little lonely. But I like having my privacy.

格蘭 : 老實說，是會有一點孤單，但是我喜歡有自己的隱私。

M　　: I know. But there were lots of good things about the dorm. Your friends are all there. And the cafeteria…

媽　　: 我明白，但是住宿舍有許多的好處。你的朋友都在那裡，而且還有自助餐…

G　　: You're still worried about me getting balanced meals? After my crash course in Cooking 101 this weekend, I'll have no problem feeding myself!

格蘭　: 你還在擔心我是否得到均衡的飲食？就在我進了 101 烹飪速成班後，我不會再有填飽肚子的問題了！

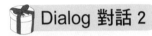 Dialog 對話 2

Jenny has driven Grant to the train station.
珍妮開車載格蘭到火車站。

J　　: I hate to say it, but it's been nice having you back this weekend.

珍妮　: 我實在很不想說肉麻話，但是這個週末你能回來真的是太好了。

G　　: I've missed you, too. You should come to Vancouver some weekend and visit me!

格蘭　: 我也很想你。你應該找個週末到溫哥華來看我。

J　　: Really? I'd love to!

珍妮　: 真的？我很樂意！

G : Cool. I can show you around all my favorite spots: We can go hiking on Grouse Mountain, check out the night market at Chinatown.

格蘭 : 太好了！ 我會帶你到我最喜歡的地方到處看看，我們可以去爬葛若斯山，逛一逛中國城的夜市。

J : And you can cook for me! I couldn't get enough of that rice you made!

珍妮 : 你還可以煮飯給我吃！你上次煮的炒飯我還吃得不過癮哩！

G : How could I refuse! How about coming over next weekend?

格蘭 : 我怎能拒絕你！下個週末來如何？

J : That sounds good. But I'll call you to make our plans. If you don't get out of the car now, you'll miss your train!

珍妮 : 聽起來不錯。我會打電話給你敲定計畫。但是如果你現在還不下車，就會趕不上火車了！

 Dialog 對話 3

Grant has just gotten home. He turns on the lights and, realizing that he is all alone, feels lonely. He walks over to his phone and checks his voice mail.

格蘭剛回家。他打開燈，就感到自己是孤零零的，很寂寞。他走到電話旁，查一查語音信箱。

Voice : You have three new messages. Message one. Friday, 3:35 pm: Hey, Grant! It's Celia. I'm not sure what you're up to this weekend, but if you're not busy tomorrow, I wanted to invite you to a party. Call me if you're interested. Bye!

答錄機 : 你有三個留言。第一個留言。星期五下午三點五十五分：嘿！格蘭，我是莎莉亞。我不知道你這個週末在做什麼，但是如果你不忙的話，我想要約你參加一場派對。如果你有興趣，請打電話給我。再見！

Voice : Message two. Saturday, 10:00 am: Hi, this is Megan. I know you're spending the weekend at your parents, but I'm not sure when you'll be back. When you get home, would you mind giving me a call? I have a question about a history assignment, and I'm hoping you can help me out!

答錄機 : 第二個留言。星期六上午十點鐘：嗨！我是梅格。我知道這個週末你和父母共聚，但我不確定你何時會回來。如果你回家了！能否請你撥個電話給我？我有歷史作業方面的問題，希望你能替我解答！

Voice : Message three. Sunday, 8:45 pm: Grant, it's your mother! I just wanted to say again how nice it was to have you home this weekend. Take good care of yourself and call us when you get in to let us know that you arrived safe and sound. We miss you!

答錄機 : 第三個留言。星期日，上午八點四十五分：格蘭，是媽媽！我只是想再說一遍，見到你這個週末回家真好。好好保重。你一進房就馬上打電話回來報平安，好讓我們知道你已經安全抵達。我們想念你！

Voice ： End of messages.

答錄機 ： 留言結束。

Useful Sentences 範例句型

All of Jenny's friends were busy, so she was all alone on Saturday night.

珍妮的所有朋友都很忙，所以週末夜晚她一個人過。

Paul wasn't sure what his friends were up to that night.

保羅不知道那天晚上他朋友都跑去做什麼了？

Where will you be spending the weekend?

你會在哪裡度週末？

Lisa was always willing to help her friends out.

麗莎總是願意幫忙她的朋友解決問題。

Vocabulary 單字片語

☑ go by — 經過

☑ by oneself — 獨自一人

☑ cafeteria — 自助餐廳

☑ balanced — 均衡的

☑ crash course — 速成課程

☑ feed — 餵食

☑ spot — 地點

☑ hiking — 健行

☑ refuse — 拒絕

☑ voice mail — 語音信箱

☑ answering machine — 答錄機

☑ pm — 下午

Chapter 3

Out and About
出門在外

Wouldn't it be nice to have somebody take care of all your chores and run all your errands for you? Imagine all the time you'd have left to study, play computer games, or just sleep! Unfortunately, most of us have to spend a lot of time out and about, running errands when we'd just rather do something else.

假如有個人可以幫我們代理一切外務、瑣碎的事，讓我們可以盡情的看書、打電玩、或是睡覺，是不是很棒呢？但不幸的是，大部分的時間，我們都要自己處理日常生活的瑣事，即使我們心裡一點兒都不情願，我們也得在外奔波繁忙。

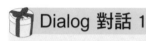

○ Track-22

🎁 Dialog 對話 1

Helen is talking to her parents.
海倫在跟父母談話。

| H | : | Mom, would it be alright if I borrowed your car this weekend? |
| 海倫 | : | 媽，我這個週末可以跟你借車嗎？ |

| M | : | What for, honey? |
| 媽 | : | 親愛的，你借車要幹麻？ |

| H | : | I want to drive to Vancouver to visit Grant. |
| 海倫 | : | 我想借開去溫哥華看格蘭。 |

| M | : | Well, I wouldn't mind, but you know how your father feels about you driving into the city. |
| 媽 | : | 嗯，我是沒問題，可是你也知道你爸不喜歡你開車去大城市。 |

I think it'd be best if you took the train.
我覺得你搭火車可能比較好。

H : But mom, the train is so crowded, and it stops running after midnight.

海倫 : 可是，火車太擠了，而且午夜後就沒車了。

M : I'm sorry. But if you like, we can drive you to the train station.

媽 : 我也很遺憾，不過假如你想的話，我們可以開車載你去車站。

H : OK, thanks. But we'd better hurry. I want to catch the express train.

海倫 : 好吧，謝謝。不過我們得趕快了。我還想趕上快車呢。

 Dialog 對話 2

Helen is at the train station talking to a ticket seller.
海倫在跟火車站售票員說話。

H : One express ticket to Vancouver, please.

海倫 : 請給我一張到溫哥華的快車票。

C : Which train, miss?

服務員 : 哪一班呢，小姐？

H : The six forty-five.

海倫 : 六點四十五分那班車。

C : I'm sorry, but we're all sold out.

服務員 : 不好意思，那班車的票全賣光了。

There's space on the seven thirty express, or you could catch the slow train at six fifty.

七點半的快車還有位子，還是你要六點五十分的慢車票呢？

H : What time does the slow train arrive in Vancouver?

海倫 : 慢車幾點會到溫哥華？

C : It will arrive at eight o'clock.

服務員 : 八點會到。

H : OK, then. One ticket to Vancouver!

海倫 : 好吧，那我要一張到溫哥華的慢車票！

 Dialog 對話 3

Helen is on the train to Vancouver. She calls Grant on his cell phone.

海倫在前往溫哥華的火車上，她打電話到格蘭的手機。

G : Hey, Helen. Are you almost here?

格蘭 : 嗨，海倫。你快到了嗎？

H : Not exactly. I had to catch the slow train, so I'll be a little late.

海倫 : 還沒，因為我搭慢車，所以會晚點到。

G : That's OK. I've got a few errands to run before you get here anyway.

格蘭 : 沒關係，在你到之前，我也有一些事情要處理。

Do you want me to pick you up from the train station?

你要我去火車站接你嗎？

H : No, that's OK. When I arrive, I'll take the bus to your place.

海倫 : 不用了，我到了再搭公車過去就好了。

G : OK. But I may be out when you arrive.

格蘭 : 好，不過你到時，我可能不在喔。

I'm going to ride my motorbike down to the market to pick up a few things.

因為我要騎車去城裡的市場買點東西。

H : No problem. If you're not home, I'll let myself in.

海倫 : 沒關係，假如你不在，我就自己進門。

I know where you've hidden your spare key.

我知道你的備份鑰匙藏在哪。

Useful Sentences 範例句型

Wendy was almost ready to go out for dinner, but she still had to put her make up on.

溫蒂已經準備好差不多可以去吃晚餐了，只差妝還沒化好而已。

My dad will catch the late bus home from work.

我爸爸下班時會趕搭末班公車回家。

Everyone was out when Sylvia got home from school today.

今天希薇亞放學回家時，家裡的人都不在。

Oliver went to the store to pick up some pens and paper.

奧立佛到店裡去買一些筆和紙。

Vocabulary 單字片語

☑ mind		介意
☑ feel		感覺
☑ be best if		最好
☑ run		跑；趕；處理
☑ midnight		午夜
☑ hurry		趕快
☑ express		快車
☑ ticket		車票
☑ sold out		賣光了
☑ errands		瑣事
☑ spare		備份

Unit 2

At the Supermarket
在超級市場

🎵 Track-23

 Dialog 對話 1

Grant has just parked his motorcycle in front of the supermarket. He goes to the produce department to find some fruit, but he can't see what he's looking for.

格蘭剛在超市門口停好機車。他到農產區去買水果，可是他找不到他想要的。

G　　: Excuse me. I'm looking for passion fruit. Do you have any?

格蘭　: 不好意思，請問你們有百香果嗎？

C　　: I'm sorry, no. Passion fruit is not in season right now.

服務員 : 抱歉，沒有，因為現在不是百香果的季節。

We do have some nice mangoes, though.
不過我們有賣好吃的芒果喔。

G　　: How much are they?

格蘭　: 芒果怎麼賣？

C　　: They're two dollars each.

服務員 : 一個二美元。

117

G : Great. Thanks.

格蘭 : 太好了，謝謝。

Say, I'm in a bit of a rush: can you tell me where I can find cheese and milk?

不好意思，我在趕時間，你可以告訴我起士跟牛奶放哪嗎？

C : Yes, those things are in the dairy aisle. I'll show you the way!

服務員 : 當然，這些都在乳製品區，我帶你去。

Dialog 對話 2

Grant's arms are full of groceries, but he still has a few more things he needs to get. He is reaching for some toilet paper, when a clerk approaches him.

格蘭手上已經抱滿了雜貨，可是他還需要再買一些東西。當他正向衛生紙前進時，一個店員走過來。

C : Excuse me, sir! You look like you've got your hands full!

服務員 : 不好意思，先生，看樣子你的手都已經拿滿東西了！

G : I'll say!

格蘭 : 看也知道！

C : Can I get you a basket?

服務員 : 需要購物籃嗎？

G : That would be great.

格蘭 : 有的話，再好不過了。

C : Here you go. Is there anything else I can help you with?

服務員 : 來，給你。還有什麼需要我幫忙的嗎？

G : As a matter of fact, yes. I have a coupon for Softy toilet paper, but I don't see any on the shelves.

格蘭 : 說真的，有，我有柔軟衛生紙的折價券，可是架子上好像沒有。

C : I'm afraid we've sold out. But I can give you a rain check.

服務員 : 可能賣完了，我下次先幫你留一份好嗎？

G : Sounds good to me, thanks.

格蘭 : 這主意不錯，謝了。

🎁 Dialog 對話 3

Grant is next at the checkout. The cashier is scanning his groceries.

格蘭在結帳櫃檯旁，店員正在幫他買的東西掃描結帳。

C : Do you have any coupons?

服務員 : 你有折價券嗎？

G : Yes, I have a coupon for the cheese.

格蘭 : 有，我有起士的折價券。

C : Thank you. Your total is twenty-two dollars; cash or charge?

服務員 : 謝謝，這樣總共是二十二美元，付現還是刷卡？

G : Cash. Here is twenty-five dollars.

格蘭 : 付現，這邊是二十五美元。

C : And here is three-dollars change.

服務員 : 找你三元。

Do you need a bag?

你需要袋子嗎？

G : No, thank you. I can just put everything in my backpack.

格蘭 : 不用，謝謝。我放背包就好。

Useful Sentences 範例句型

Bruce showed his son how to ride a bicycle last year.

布魯斯去年教他兒子騎腳踏車。

Rick's hands were full, so he had to ask his wife to open the door for him.

瑞克的手提滿了東西，所以他請他太太幫他開門。

The total of the bill came to over two hundred dollars.

帳單總金額都快到二百美金了。

Lily's backpack was very heavy because it was full of books.

麗莉的背包很重，因為裡面放滿了書本。

Vocabulary 單字片語

☑ park		停車
☑ in front of		在…前面
☑ produce		產品；農產品
☑ department		部門
☑ fruit		水果
☑ look for something		找尋某物
☑ passion fruit		百香果
☑ in season		當季
☑ mango		芒果
☑ each		每一個
☑ be in a rush		趕時間
☑ dairy		乳製品
☑ aisle		走道
☑ basket		籃子

☑ coupon 折價券

☑ toilet paper 衛生紙

☑ shelf 架子

☑ rain check 預留

☑ scan 掃描

☑ cashier 收銀員

☑ cash 現金

☑ charge 收費

☑ backpack 背包

MEMO

Unit
3
At the Cleaners

在洗衣店

Track-24

 Dialog 對話 1

Grant and Helen have just finished dinner at Grant's apartment.

格蘭跟海倫在家裡吃完晚餐。

H : That was a great dinner, Grant!
海倫 : 格蘭，今天的菜真是太棒了！

Your cooking skills have really come a long way!
你的廚藝真是沒話說！

G : You have my mother to thank!
格蘭 : 你應該感謝我媽！

She taught me everything I know. More wine?
這些都是她教我的，還要酒嗎？

H : Yes, please. Aaack!
海倫 : 好，麻煩你了。唉呀！

G : Oh, Helen! I'm sorry! I'm so clumsy.
格蘭 : 喔！對不起！我真是太笨手笨腳了。

123

Let me go get a towel.
我幫你拿一條毛巾來。

H : My new dress! This wine will never come out!
海倫 : 我的洋裝！這些酒漬一定洗不掉了！

G : Don't worry. You can change into one of my t-shirts and a pair of shorts.
格蘭 : 別擔心。你可以先換我的 T 恤跟短褲穿。

I'll try to wash this, and by the time you go home, your dress will be as good as new!
我會想辦法洗乾淨的，等你要回家時，洋裝就會跟新的一樣！

 Dialog 對話 2

The next day, Helen is at the dry cleaners speaking to a clerk.
隔天，海倫在乾洗店跟一位員工說話。

C : Can I help you?
服務員 : 需要我幫忙嗎？

H : Yes. I need this dress dry cleaned.
海倫 : 是的，我想要乾洗這件洋裝。

C : Are there any stains that need attention?
服務員 : 有任何需要特殊處裡的污漬嗎？

H　　：Yes. There's a wine stain across the front.

海倫　：有，前面有一道酒漬。

Do you think you can get it out?

你想這洗的掉嗎？

My boyfriend tried, but he didn't have any luck.

我男朋友試過了，可是他洗不掉。

C　　：Hmm. This won't be easy, but I think I know just what will do the trick.

服務員　：嗯，可能會有點困難，不過我們知道處理方法。

When would you like to pick the dress up?

你什麼時候要來拿衣服？

H　　：Is it possible to have it by Wednesday?

海倫　：禮拜三可以嗎？

C　　：Wednesday? No problem!

服務員　：禮拜三？沒問題！

 Dialog 對話 3

On Wednesday, Helen returns to the dry-cleaners to get her dress.

禮拜三，海倫去乾洗店拿洋裝。

H　　：I'm here to pick up my dress.

海倫　：我是來拿我的洋裝的。

C : Ah yes, let me go get it...Here it is.

服務員 : 啊對，我拿給你。這邊。

H : Wow, this looks terrific! The stain is completely gone!

海倫 : 哇，看起來太棒了！污漬完全不見了！

C : I was a little surprised at how well it turned out myself.

服務員 : 我自己也很驚訝這種神奇的效果。

H : Outside, your sign says that your business does alterations as well as dry cleaning.

海倫 : 外面的招牌説，你這邊除了乾洗也有修改衣服的服務。

C : That's right. Do you need anything altered?

服務員 : 沒錯，你有要改衣服嗎？

H : Yes. I'd like to have these pants hemmed.

海倫 : 對，我想把這件褲子改短。

When can you do it by?

你什麼時候可以做？

C : I'm not sure. Let me go to the back room and check with our tailor.

服務員 : 我不確定。我進去問一下裁縫師。

Useful Sentences 範例句型

After taking his medicine, the sick man felt as good as new.

吃了藥之後，這位病人馬上感覺跟新生一樣。

Kim bought a shirt with a picture of a dragon across the front.

金買了件前面畫了一條龍的襯衫。

Adding a little salt to the sauce will do the trick!

在洗劑裡加點鹽，就能產生神奇功效！

Iris checked with her parents to see if it was OK for her to go to the movies.

愛芮思問她父母可不可以去看電影。

Vocabulary 單字片語

☑ come a long way	其來有自
☑ wine	酒
☑ clumsy	笨手笨腳
☑ towel	毛巾
☑ come out	清出來
☑ pair of	成雙的
☑ shorts	短褲
☑ dry clean	乾洗

☑	stain	污漬
☑	across	穿過
☑	terrific	棒極了
☑	turn out	結果
☑	alterations	修改
☑	hem	裁短
☑	tailor	裁縫師

MEMO

Unit 4

The Mechanic
修車記

 Track-25

 Dialog 對話 1

Helen is on her way back home from the dry cleaners. She is driving her parents' car, when suddenly she hears a strange noise and the car dies.

海倫正準備從乾洗店回家，她開著她爸媽的車，突然一陣奇響，車子停止發動了。

H   : Dad?
海倫   : 爸，是你嗎？

D   : Yes, Helen. What is it?
爸   : 對，海倫，怎麼了？

H   : I'm sorry to tell you this, but the car has broken down.
海倫   : 我跟你說個壞消息，車子拋錨不動了。

         It made a strange noise, and then it stopped moving.
         它發出一聲怪聲，然後就停止發動了。

D   : Have you tried starting it up again?
爸   : 你有試著再發動一次嗎？

H　　：Yes, but it isn't responding.

海倫　：有，可是沒反應。

D　　：Where are you?

爸　　：你現在哪兒？

H　　：I'm at the corner of Main Street and First Avenue.

海倫　：我在主線跟第一大道交界處。

D　　：Alright. Wait there, and I'll call a tow truck to take you to the nearest service station.

爸　　：好，你先等著，我打電話請最近的拖吊服務去接你。

 Dialog 對話 2

Helen is at the service station talking to a mechanic.

海倫在拖吊維修中心與技術人員說話。

H　　：What do you think the problem is?

海倫　：你覺得問題出在哪？

M　　：I'm not entirely sure right now, but I think I may need to replace a few parts in your engine.

技工　：我不確定，我想可能要先把你引擎換掉看看。

H　　：When do you think you'll be able to have the repairs done by?

海倫　：那你應該要什麼時候才能把引擎問題修好？

M : Well, we're pretty busy today, so we may not have a chance to fix everything until tomorrow or the next day.

技工 : 這個嘛，我們今天滿忙的，所以可能要到明後天才可以全修好。

H : OK. But before you begin, can you please call me on my cell phone and give me an estimate on how much the cost will be?

海倫 : 好吧，那可不以請你要動工前，先打我手機通知我一下大概的花費？

M : No problem. Just write your phone number down here, and I'll call you as soon as I know.

技工 : 沒問題，請你留個電話號碼，我一找出毛病馬上通知你。

🎁 Dialog 對話 3

Helen is at home when her phone rings. It's the mechanic.

當電話響起時，海倫正在家。是那位技術人員打來的。

M : Hello, this is Jim Liu from Swifty Auto Repairs.

技工 : 哈囉，我是史威提汽車修理廠的吉姆。

I'm calling about your vehicle, the 2000 Honda Accord.

我是為了你的本田車打來的。

H : Yes. Do you know what the problem is, yet?

海倫 : 是的，你知道問題出在哪了嗎？

M : Yes. The problem was simply overheating.

技工 : 是的，問題很簡單，只是引擎過熱而已。

Your engine lacked sufficient coolant.

你的引擎冷卻劑不夠。

We'll replace it, and do some routine maintenance.

我們會把它換掉，再做一些日常保養。

H : That's great news! How much will that cost?

海倫 : 這樣就太好了！這要花多少錢？

M : Sixty dollars. Your car will be ready to be picked up tomorrow.

技工 : 六十美元。你明天就可以來拿車。

H : Super! My dad will be very pleased to hear this. Thank you!

海倫 : 耶！我爸會很高興聽到這個消息。謝謝你！

Useful Sentences 範例句型

Andy was so busy at work that he didn't have a chance to take a break.

安迪工作太忙，所以沒有時間休息一下。

Does the doctor have any idea what the problem with Julie's health is?

醫生知道茱麗健康哪裡出問題了嗎？

Johnny didn't have enough money to buy a new bike.

強尼沒有錢可以買新腳踏車。

The reporters wrote down everything the man was saying.

記者寫下了這個人所說的每句話。

Vocabulary 單字片語

☐	be on one's way	在…路上
☐	break down	拋錨
☐	strange	奇怪的
☐	respond	回應
☐	avenue	大道
☐	tow truck	拖吊車
☐	nearest	最近的
☐	service station	維修服務處
☐	mechanic	技術人員；技工
☐	entirely	完全地
☐	replace	取代；換掉

- ☑ engine 引擎
- ☑ repair 修理
- ☑ estimate 估價
- ☑ lack 缺乏
- ☑ coolant 冷卻劑
- ☑ routine 慣例
- ☑ maintenance 保養

MEMO

Unit 5

At the Department Store

到百貨公司

 Track-26

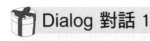 Dialog 對話 1

It's almost Helen's birthday. Grant is at the department store with Megan looking for a present for her.

海倫的生日快到了。格蘭跟梅格一起到百貨公司幫她選禮物。

G : Thanks for agreeing to come with me! I never know what to get people for their birthdays.

格蘭 : 謝謝你答應陪我來！關於生日禮物方面，我總是一點主意也沒有。

M : No problem. I love shopping! But where should we start?

梅格 : 別客氣，我喜歡逛街買東西！我們該從那兒開始呢？

Do you have any idea what kind of gift you'd like to get for Helen?

你有想買給海倫的東西嗎？

G : Well, I was thinking of some cosmetics.

格蘭 : 嗯，我有想到一些保養品。

I know she likes SKII products and...

我知道她喜歡 SKII 的東西…

135

M　　：Unless it's perfume, forget it!

梅格　：除非是香水，不然就不要！

　　　　Buying Helen cosmetics will send the wrong message.

　　　　送海倫保養品會讓她誤以為你對她的外表有意見。

G　　：Like, "You're not pretty enough the way you are"?

格蘭　：你是說，她會認為我嫌她不夠漂亮？

　　　　I guess that wouldn't make her birthday very happy.

　　　　這樣她生日就會不開心了。

　　　　Let's skip the cosmetics department then.

　　　　那就不要送保養品好了。

M　　：And head straight to the clothing department.

梅格　：那麼直接去服飾部吧。

　　　　I'm sure she'd love something in women's wear!

　　　　我想她一定會喜歡跟女裝相關的東西！

🎁 Dialog 對話 2

Grant and Megan have just stepped off the escalator, and are heading into one of the women's boutiques.

格蘭跟梅格走完手扶電梯，向女裝部前進。

M　　：Hmm. This dress is nice. Red would look nice on Helen.

梅格　：嗯，這洋裝不錯，海倫滿適合穿紅色的。

G	:	You're right, but it's too short. She'd never wear it.
格蘭	:	你說的對，可是這件太短了。她絕對不會穿的。

M	:	How about this sweater?
梅格	:	那這件毛衣怎麼樣？

It's conservative and it's on sale!
這就保守多了，而且這件在特價！

G	:	It's nice...but not special enough for a birthday gift.
格蘭	:	是不錯，可是…拿來當生日禮物不夠特別。

M	:	So you want something a little more romantic, huh?
梅格	:	那你是想買浪漫一點的東西囉？

Well, I guess we could just walk on over to the lingerie department and see what's there!
嗯，我想我們乾脆去逛逛女用內衣，看看那邊有什麼好貨色。

G	:	Hey! I want to get her something she won't feel embarrassed to show her family when they ask what her boyfriend's present was.
格蘭	:	嘿！我想買的是，她可以大方跟家人展示的禮物。

M	:	Only one more option then : jewelry!
梅格	:	那就只有一個選擇了－首飾！

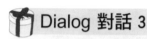 Dialog 對話 3

Grant and Megan have just picked out a nice pair of gold and diamond earrings for Helen. The salesgirl is wrapping them for Grant.

格蘭跟梅格選了一付黃金鑲鑽耳環給海倫。女店員幫格蘭包裝禮物。

M ： Make sure that you keep the receipt, Grant.
梅格 ： 格蘭，你要把收據收好。

G ： Of course! I always keep the receipt.
格蘭 ： 當然，我總是會把收據收著的。

M ： If you keep your receipt, then you will be able to return the earrings if Helen doesn't like them.
梅格 ： 我是說你把收據收好，這樣到時假如海倫不喜歡，你還可以拿來退還。

G ： If Helen doesn't like them?
格蘭 ： 假如海倫不喜歡？
You're freaking me out, Meg.
你在整我啊。
Do you think the diamonds are too small?
你覺得這鑽石太小了？
Are the earrings the wrong shape?
還是這個耳環形狀不好？
Oh my goodness, this is a big mistake!
喔，我的天啊，真是個天大的錯誤！

M : Cool it, Grant! The earrings are perfect.

梅格 : 冷靜一點！這耳環很好。

Forget I said anything.
當我沒説吧。

G : OK. Because I'm counting on diamonds being a girl's best friend and mine!

格蘭 : 好。雖然鑽石是你們女生最好的朋友，現在也是我的了！

Useful Sentences 範例句型

Jerry never knew how to fix his computer, so he always had to ask his friends to help him.

傑瑞從來不知道該拿他的電腦怎麼辦，所以他總得請朋友幫他解決電腦問題。

That's a nice pair of shoes that you're wearing!

你穿的鞋子好好看啊！

When Susan fell while walking down the street, she was very embarrassed.

蘇珊走路時滑了一跤，讓她覺得很丟臉。

During the test, Sam realized that it had been a big mistake to watch TV the night before instead of studying.

考試時，山姆才領悟到考前不抱佛腳，抱電視是個天大的錯誤。

Vocabulary 單字片語

☑	present	禮物
☑	agree	同意
☑	start	開始
☑	cosmetics	化妝品；保養品
☑	perfume	香水
☑	send somebody a message	暗示；隱喻
☑	skip something	略過
☑	head to/for/in	朝；向
☑	straight	直接
☑	escalator	手扶電梯
☑	conservative	保守的
☑	on sale	特價中
☑	romantic	浪漫的
☑	lingerie	女用內衣
☑	jewelry	珠寶首飾
☑	diamond	鑽石
☑	earring	耳環
☑	receipt	收據
☑	freak somebody out	找麻煩
☑	count on somebody/something	仰賴；計算

🎁 Dialog 對話 1

Megan is going to the bank to open an account. She takes a number, and goes to a teller when it's her turn.

梅格到銀行開戶頭。當輪到她時,她跟銀行行員說話。

M	:	Hello. I'd like to open an account!
梅格	:	哈囉,我想開戶頭!

T	:	Checking or savings?
行員	:	劃撥還是存款戶頭?

M	:	A savings account.
梅格	:	存款戶頭。

T	:	Do you have any identification?
行員	:	您有帶身分證件嗎?

M	:	Yes. Here you are.
梅格	:	有的,這裡。

T	:	How much money would you like to deposit into the account?
行員	:	您想先存多少錢進去?

M : I have three hundred dollars, cash, and a check for five hundred.

梅格 : 我有三百元現金跟一張五百元支票。

T : Just a moment, please.

行員 : 請您稍候一下。

The clerk runs the money through the counting machine).
（行員將金錢放到點鈔機數過）

🎁 Dialog 對話 2

A few minutes later, the teller returns.
過一會，行員回來。

T : I just need your signature on this form, please.

行員 : 我需要您在這份表格上簽個名。

M : OK. Is there anything else I need to do?

梅格 : 好，這樣就好了嗎？

T : No. This is your passbook.

行員 : 不，這是您的存摺簿。

Bring it with you every time you need to deposit money into your account, and we'll update it to show all your transactions.

當您要存款時，記得把本子帶過來，我們會把所有交易明細都記錄進去。

M 　 : Great. But does this account come with an automatic teller card?

梅格 　 : 太好了，請問這個戶頭有沒有提款卡呢？

T 　 : Yes. Here it is.

行員 　 : 有，這邊。

You can go to one of the ATMs downstairs and change your personal identification number there.

您可以到樓下的自動提款機，先把個人的密碼重新設定過。

But remember one important thing:

有一件很重要的事您一定要記得。

Never tell anyone your PIN!

千萬不可以跟別人説您的登入密碼！

M 　 : Check!

梅格 　 : 我知道了！

 Dialog 對話 3

Megan and Kurt have just finished eating lunch. She has realized that she is short of cash.

梅格跟科特才剛吃完午餐，梅格就發現她錢沒帶夠。

M 　 : Darn it! I was just at the bank today, and I forgot to withdraw enough money to get me through the week.

梅格 　 : 可惡！我剛去銀行，卻忘了留一個禮拜的生活費在身上。

K   : No problem. This is my treat!
科特   : 沒關係。這次我請客！

M   : No, no, you paid last time.
梅格   : 不用，不用，你上次請過我了。

I think there's an ATM nearby.
我想這附近應該有自動提款機。

I'll be back in second.
我去找一下，馬上回來。

K   : Wait!
科特   : 等等！

You shouldn't just take money out of the ATM whenever you feel like it!
你不應該隨心所欲，愛提錢就提錢！

M   : Why not? It's convenient.
梅格   : 為什麼不行？這樣很方便啊。

K   : Yes, but every time you withdraw money, you have to pay a fee.
科特   : 沒錯，可是你每提一次錢，就要付一次手續費。

Over time that can add up.
久了就是一筆大數目了。

M   : I guess I should plan my spending more carefully.
梅格   : 我想我應該更慎重盤算一下我的支出了。

K　　　: Right. And plan on treating me, next time!

科特　　: 沒錯。記得把該回請我的也盤算進去！

Useful Sentences 範例句型

It is important to recycle because the waste we make adds up.

因為我們浪費的東西增多，因此回收工作就顯得相形重要。

Since it's your birthday, you don't need to worry about paying, it's my treat!

既然今天是你生日，你就不用擔心付帳的事，我請客！

To join this gym, you need to pay a fee each month.

你要繳交月費，才能加入健身俱樂部。

Johnny was a poor student at first, but over time, his grades improved.

剛開始強尼的成績很差，但時間久了，成績就進步了。

Vocabulary 單字片語

☑ teller	銀行行員
☑ open an account	開戶頭
☑ account	戶頭
☑ checking	劃撥

☑	savings	存款
☑	deposit	存錢
☑	cash	現金
☑	check	支票
☑	run through	處理
☑	counting machine	點鈔機
☑	signature	簽名
☑	form	表格
☑	passbook	存摺
☑	update	更新
☑	transaction	交易
☑	automatic teller card	提款卡
☑	atm (automatic teller machine)	自動提款機
☑	withdraw	提出

Track-28

 Dialog 對話 1

Megan has dropped by Grant's place. She notices that he looks blue.

梅格順道到格蘭的住處。她發現格蘭看起來有點沮喪。

M : Grant, are you OK? You don't look very happy.

梅格 : 格蘭,你還好吧?看起有點不開心。

G : Oh, I'm OK. It's just those earrings that I bought for Megan...

格蘭 : 喔,我還好,只是買給海倫的那付耳環…

M : Don't tell me she didn't like them! Well, at least you saved the receipt!

梅格 : 別跟我說海倫不喜歡!就算這樣,你也還有收據吧!

G : Megan! That's not it. I just got my credit card bill for them.

格蘭 : 梅格!不是這個。我只是收到耳環的信用卡帳單。

M : I see. I remember they weren't cheap.

梅格 : 這樣啊,我記得應該不便宜吧。

G   : They weren't. And now I've got a huge bill to pay!

格蘭   : 不便宜。現在我有一大筆帳單要付了！

 ## Dialog 對話 2

Megan has noticed a big stack of papers and envelopes on Grant's desk.

梅格發現格蘭書桌上有一疊單據、信封。

M   : What are all those?

梅格   : 這些是什麼啊？

G   : Bills, bills, bills.

格蘭   : 帳單、帳單、帳單。

Telephone bill, electricity bill, a bill for my tuition, another credit card bill, and some others.

電話費、電費、學費、卡費、還有一些其他的。

M   : Grant, you can't just let them sit on the desk collecting dust!

梅格   : 格蘭，你不能就讓這些單子在桌上長灰塵啊！

That'll affect your credit rating!

這樣會影響你的信用額度的！

G   : I know, but I'm so busy with school and work, I don't have enough time to go and pay them all.

格蘭   : 我知道，可是我學校跟工作都忙，根本沒時間去付清所有帳單。

M : You're just lazy.

梅格 : 你是懶惰。

Everyone knows you can pay most of your bills at 7-Eleven.

誰都知道你可以去便利商店繳費。

And the others you can mail in with your payment.

其他的你也可以用匯款方式付清啊。

G : You're right. I have no excuse.

格蘭 : 你說的對。是我不好。

Tomorrow I'll pay all my bills!

明天我就會去把帳單付清！

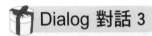 Dialog 對話 3

Grant is at 7-Eleven.

格蘭在便利商店。

G : Excuse me. I'd like to pay my telephone and electricity bills.

格蘭 : 不好意思，我想繳電話費跟電費。

Can I do that here?

我可以在這邊繳嗎？

C : Sure can. I just need to scan them first.

服務員 : 當然，只要讓我掃描讀取一下就好了。

G	:	Here you go.
格蘭	:	這裡。

C	:	OK. The total will be seventy-five dollars.
服務員	:	好，一共是七十五美元。

G	:	Easy for you to say. Here's one hundred.
格蘭	:	你說的輕鬆，來，這是一百元。

C	:	And twenty-five is your change.
服務員	:	這是找你的二十五元。

Just a moment while I stamp them...
我蓋個章，請等一下。

OK, this portion is for you to keep in your records.
好了，這收據給你以後查證用。

G	:	Great, thanks. This was totally convenient.
格蘭	:	太棒了，謝謝，真是夠便利的了。

C	:	That's what we're here for!
服務員	:	這就是我們的目的啊！

Useful Sentences 範例句型

Sam didn't use his college textbooks anymore, they just sat on a shelf collecting dust.

山姆已經再也用不著大學教科書，那些書都堆在架上生灰塵。

Marsha had no excuse for failing the test.

瑪莎考試失敗其實是她自己的錯。

I have to get two teeth pulled by the dentist?! Easy for you to say!

我得讓牙醫拔兩顆牙！？你說得倒輕鬆！

Please, don't thank me for listening to you. You're my friend. Listening is what I'm here for.

好啦，不用謝我啦。我們是朋友，我當然很樂意傾聽你的心聲。

Vocabulary 單字片語

☑	pay bills	支付帳單
☑	earrings	耳環
☑	cheap	便宜的
☑	huge	巨大的
☑	stack	堆；疊
☑	envelope	信封
☑	electricity	電力
☑	telephone	電話
☑	credit rating	信用額度
☑	payment	付款
☑	scan something	掃描
☑	stamp	蓋印
☑	portion	收據
☑	records	紀錄

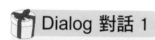 Dialog 對話 1

Grant is at the post office. He needs to mail a bill, an international letter, and a parcel.

格蘭在郵局。他要寄匯票、航空信,跟一個包裹。

C	: Can I help you?
服務員	: 需要我幫忙嗎?

G	: Yes, I'd like to mail a bill.
格蘭	: 是的,我想寄張匯票。

C	: Is it local or international?
服務員	: 本地還是國際?

G	: Local.
格蘭	: 本地。

C	: Would you like it to be delivered promptly?
服務員	: 你需要快遞送達嗎?

G	: No. It's not that urgent.
格蘭	: 不用,沒那麼趕。

C　　　: OK. A stamp will cost you forty-five cents.

服務員 : 好，那麼郵資是五十五分。

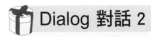 **Dialog 對話 2**

Grant tells the clerk he also has an international letter that he wants to mail.

格蘭跟辦事員說他還有一封航空信要寄。

C　　　: What is the destination?

服務員 : 要寄到哪？

G　　　: England. My friend is studying there!

格蘭　 : 英國，我朋友在那唸書！

C　　　: The price depends on how much it weighs.

服務員 : 郵資要看重量決定。

　　　　 May I have your letter please?

　　　　 可以麻煩把信件給我嗎？

G　　　: Here it is.

格蘭　 : 這裡。

C　　　: Thank you. Alright, that will cost seventy cents.

服務員 : 謝謝，好，這樣是七十分錢。

G　　　: Can you deliver it airmail?

格蘭　 : 會用航空寄嗎？

C   : Certainly, anything else?

服務員 ： 當然，還需要什麼嗎？

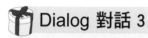 Dialog 對話 3

Grant holds up a parcel.
格蘭拿出一個包裹。

C   : And where are you sending your package to?

服務員 ： 這個包裹你要寄到哪呢？

G   : To White Rock, please. I'd take it myself, but I don't have time.

格蘭 ： 到白石鎮，麻煩你了。我本想自己送，可是我又沒時間。

C   : I need to weigh it please. Thank you.

服務員 ： 麻煩讓我秤一下重。謝謝。

This will cost twenty dollars.
這樣是二十元。

G   : Great. When will it arrive?

格蘭 ： 好，那什麼時候送到？

C   : In approximately two days.

服務員 ： 應該兩天左右。

Would you like to send this by registered mail?
還是你要寄限時專送？

G   : I would. I don't want the box to get lost
         somewhere along the way.

格蘭   : 好，因為我擔心沿途包裹會寄丟。

C   : Registered mail will be a little more expensive.

服務員 : 限時專送會貴一點喔。

G   : That's OK. I don't mind splurging.

格蘭   : 沒關係，花點錢我還可以接受。

Useful Sentences 範例句型

Thank you, but I don't need any help. I can do it myself.

> 謝謝你，我不需要任何幫助。我自己來就可以了。

I saw lots of interesting things along my way.

> 沿途上我看到很多有趣的東西。

I'm still hungry. Can I have a little more ice cream, please?

> 我還沒飽，可以再給我一些冰淇淋嗎？

The train will leave in approximately twenty minutes.

> 火車大概二十分鐘後開動。

Vocabulary 單字片語

☑ post office — 郵局

☑ parcel — 包裹

☑ international — 國際的

☑ deliver — 寄送

☑ promptly — 快速地

☑ urgent — 緊急的

☑ stamp — 郵票；郵資

☑ destination — 目的地

☑ weigh — 重量

☑ airmail — 航空信

☑ hold something up — 拿出

☑ approximately — 約略地

☑ registered mail — 限時專送

☑ splurge — 花錢

Unit 9

Home Repair

整修

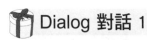 Dialog 對話 1

Grant is at home and his phone rings. It's his sister calling.

格蘭在家裡，電話響了。是他姊姊打來的。

I   : Grant? It's Iris!

愛芮思 : 格蘭？我是愛芮思！

G   : Hey, sis! Did you get my package yet?

格蘭 : 嗨，姊！你收到我的包裹了嗎？

I   : That's why I'm calling!

愛芮思 : 這就是打給你的目的啊！

It's so good of you to remember my birthday!

真高興你記得我生日！

And to remember that I'm doing some home repair…

而且你還知道我在整修房子…

G   : I thought you'd appreciate some tools.

格蘭 : 我想你會需要些工具的。

Not a usual birthday gift, but I figured a hammer and a screw driver would come in handy.

雖然拿來當生日禮物有點不尋常，我還是覺得一把槌子跟一些螺絲起子對你是比較實用的。

157

I : You figured right.

愛芮思 : 你的設想是對的。

I've already used the screw driver to tighten the hinges around one of my doors, and the hammer to put some nails in the wall to hang a picture.

我已經用螺絲起子把門閂鎖緊，還用槌子釘些釘子來掛圖片呢。

G : Wow, it sounds like there's a lot to do around your house.

格蘭 : 哇，聽起來你家在做很大的工程呢。

I guess I'm lucky to have a landlord.

雖然我沒有自己的房子，但有個房東也不錯。

If anything needs to be fixed, I can count on him to do it!

任何需要修理的事，我都可以仰賴他呢！

🎁 Dialog 對話 2

Grant is in the shower when suddenly the hot water turns off. He gets out and dries off angrily. He decides to call his landlord.

格蘭？澡到一半，突然沒熱水了。他生氣地走出浴室，把自己擦乾。他決定打個電話給房東。

G : Hello. My name is Grant. I'm Mr. Lin's tenant in Vancouver.

格蘭 : 哈囉，我是格蘭，我是林先生溫哥華的房客。

W : Hello. Mr. Lin isn't home right now, but maybe I can help you?

吳小姐 : 嗨，你好，林先生不在家，有什麼事，或許我可以幫忙？

I'm his wife, Miss Wu.

我是他太太，我姓吳。

G : Alright. I was just in the shower and the hot water stopped working.

格蘭 : 好吧，我剛？澡到一半，可是熱水卻沒了。

W : It sounds like you might need to call a plumber.

吳小姐 : 聽起來或許你需要請個水電工。

G : Can't Mr. Lin come over and take a look?

格蘭 : 林先生不能過來看一下嗎？

Plumbers are expensive.

水電工很貴的。

W : I'm sorry, but Mr. Lin is on a business trip right now.

吳小姐 : 很抱歉，林先生現在出差中。

I'll have him call you when he gets back, though.

等他回來，我會告訴你來過電話的。

G : When will that be?

格蘭 : 那要等到什麼時候？

W   : Next week.

吳小姐 : 下禮拜喔。

 Dialog 對話 3

Grant calls his parents and is asking his mother for advice.

格蘭打電話給他爸媽，尋求建議。

M   : No hot water, huh?

媽   : 又沒熱水啦？

G   : Nope. I guess I should just bite the bullet and call a plumber.

格蘭   : 對啊，我想我應該就算了，直接請水電工來。

I can't very well go without a shower for a week!

我總不能一個禮拜都不洗澡吧！

M   : Not so quick. Maybe you can solve this problem on your own.

媽   : 先別這麼說，說不定你可以自己解決這個問題啊。

Is your water heated by gas or electricity?

你的熱水器是瓦斯還是電力的？

G   : Gas. Why?

格蘭   : 瓦斯的，怎樣？

M	: You probably have a problem with the heater.
媽	: 説不定只是熱水器壞了。
	My guess is that your gas tank has run dry, or that the battery that keeps the heater going has died.
	我想説不定你瓦斯沒了，不然就是熱水器電池沒電了吧。

G	: So fixing my problem may simply be a matter of getting more gas, or replacing the battery?
格蘭	: 就是説，我只要換個瓦斯或電池，就可以解決我的問題？

M	: Right.
媽	: 對。
	You'd better check, before wasting time and money on an expensive repairman.
	在花大錢請人來修之前，我建議你先檢查一下。

Useful Sentences 範例句型

It would be good of you to water my plants while I'm away.

假如我不在時，你能幫我替植物澆花，那就太好了。

My keychain has a pair of scissors on it. They come in handy when I need to cut something!

我的鑰匙圈上有附一把剪刀，這樣我需要剪東西時，就隨時有工具可用。

Whenever I need help, I can always count on my parents.

每當我需要幫助時，我總是可以信賴我的父母。

Greta asked her sister for some good advice.

葛芮塔向她姊姊尋求一些好的建議。

Vocabulary 單字片語

☑ repair		修理
☑ sis		姊妹
☑ appreciate		感謝；喜歡
☑ usual		尋常的
☑ figure		想；思忖
☑ tool		工具
☑ hammer		槌子
☑ screwdriver		螺絲起子
☑ tighten		鎖緊
☑ hinge		門閂
☑ nail		釘子
☑ hang		掛
☑ shower		洗澡
☑ turn something off/on		關掉
☑ angrily		生氣地

☑ dry something off	擦乾
☑ plumber	水電工
☑ replace	取代
☑ battery	電池
☑ repairman	修理人員

MEMO

....

....

....

....

....

....

....

....

....

....

....

Chapter 4

SOS!

求救！

We all try to be independent in our lives, it's part of being an adult. Sometimes, however, life throws something unexpected in our paths. Whether it's a small matter or a life-threatening one, we all need to know when to ask for help, and how to give it when others need a hand.

我們總是在追求獨立自主的生活，而這也是成人世界的一部分。可是有時候，天外飛來一筆我們沒料到的事，不論大事小事，我們總得知道向誰求助，也得學會在別人需要幫助時，適時伸出援手。

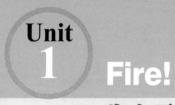

Unit 1 Fire!

失火了！

 Dialog 對話 1

Grant is home visiting his family for the weekend. He is in the kitchen cooking and calls to his mother.

格蘭週末回家跟家人聚會。他在廚房煮東西煮到一半時，喊了他媽媽。

G : Hey mom, can you pass me the Soy sauce?

格蘭 : 嘿，媽，把醬油給我好嗎？

M : It's in the pantry, dear!

媽 : 就在食物儲藏室裡！

G : I get the hint! I'll get it myself.

格蘭 : 喔，我知道了！我自己拿。

I can't see it, mom!

媽，我找不到！

M : It's on the bottom shelf, to the left, beside the rice bin.

媽 : 在最底層，左邊，米缸旁邊。

G : Still can't see it. Are you sure it's there?

格蘭 : 還是沒有。你確定放在那邊？

M : Grant? I smell smoke!

媽 : 格蘭？我聞到煙味！

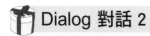 Dialog 對話 2

Grant steps out of the pantry and sees that there's a fire on the stove.

格蘭走出儲藏室，他看到爐子起火了。

G : Fire! Call the fire department!

格蘭 : 失火了！快打電話給消防隊！

M : It's not an emergency…yet.

媽 : 應該還不是很緊急…吧。

　　　Just stay calm and we'll put it out.

　　　冷靜下來，我們可以把火撲滅的。

G : Right, right. Where's the fire extinguisher?

格蘭 : 好好，滅火器在那兒？

　　　What are you doing?

　　　你在幹什麼？

M : The best way to stop a grease fire is to smother it by putting a lid on the pot.

媽 : 要滅油火的最好方法就是找個蓋子把鍋子蓋起來。

Now you turn off the stove.

好，現在你把火關掉。

G : Whew. I'm glad we got that under control.

格蘭 : 呼，太好了，幸好情況控制住了。

M : So am I!

媽 : 我也這麼覺得！

🎁 Dialog 對話 3

Grant's family has decided to have dinner at a restaurant. Grant's sister, Peggy, is bugging her brother, and their father interrupts.

格蘭家決定到外面餐廳吃飯。格蘭的妹妹珮姬正在纏著他的哥哥，爸爸出面制止。

F : The lesson to learn here is that food on the stove should never be left unattended.

爸 : 這件事給我們一個教訓就是，當爐子上在煮東西時，人千萬不能走開。

P : That's right! But dad, I'm worried about something.

珮姬 : 沒錯！爸爸，我擔心一件事。

F : What's that?

爸 : 什麼事？

| P | : | Well, we live in a big apartment building, and there are dozens of other families, and I'm sure that some of them have had problems like this. |
| 珮姬 | : | 嗯，我們住在一棟公寓裡，或許其他人家也會發生類似的事呢。 |

| F | : | That's right. |
| 爸 | : | 有可能。 |

P	:	But what if somebody has a fire and they aren't able to put it out quickly or easily?
珮姬	:	那假如別人家著火，他們又不能趕快撲滅，那怎麼辦？
		Not only would they be hurt, but likely their neighbors would be too.
		這樣不只他們受傷，連鄰居也會遭殃呢。

| F | : | That's why it's everybody's responsibility to make sure that their sprinklers work, and that their smoke detectors are functioning. |
| 爸 | : | 這就是為什麼每個人都該確保家裡灑水器跟感煙警報器都正常運作的原因了。 |

Useful Sentences 範例句型

Martin told his sister that he would get the phone himself.

馬汀跟他姊姊說，他要自己接電話。

The supervisor told his workers to move the machine a little to the right.

主管要求工人把機器右移一點。

To save water, be sure to turn off the water while you are brushing your teeth.

當你刷牙時，記得把水關掉，這樣才省水。

There are dozens of ways to help the earth; recycling is one of them!

拯救地球有很多方法，資源回收就是其一。

Vocabulary 單字片語

☑ Soya sauce	醬油
☑ pantry	食物儲藏室
☑ dear	親愛的
☑ hint	暗示
☑ bottom	底部
☑ shelf	架子
☑ smoke	煙
☑ step out	走出
☑ fire	火
☑ fire department	消防隊
☑ emergency	緊急事件

☑ calm		冷靜的
☑ put sth. out		撲滅
☑ grease		油脂
☑ fire extinguisher		滅火器
☑ lid		蓋子
☑ pot		鍋子
☑ be under control		在控制中
☑ bug		煩鬧
☑ interrupt		制止；打斷
☑ responsibility		責任
☑ function		運作
☑ sprinkler		灑水器

MEMO

....

....

....

....

....

....

....

Keeping Safe at Home
居家安全

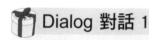 Dialog 對話 1

Back at home, Grant and his sister discuss safety.
回家後，格蘭跟妹妹討論安全的事。

G	:	You've got me thinking about how safe our home is.
格蘭	:	你讓我想起居家安全的問題。
		How about we take a look around and make sure that everything is up to snuff?
		我們檢查一下家裡，看看是不是一切都很安全，你說怎樣？
P	:	Good idea. We can start in the kitchen.
珮姬	:	好主意。我們先從廚房開始吧。
		Well, there's the first thing we need to do.
		我覺得那是第一個該檢查的地方。
G	:	Put new batteries in the smoke detector.
格蘭	:	先把感煙警報器的電池換新。
		I noticed that it hadn't gone off when I had my little accident.
		我發現在之前那個小意外發生時，它並沒有響。

P : Let me put that on my list of things to do. Batteries.

珮姬 : 那我就把它記在名單上：電池。

What else?

還有呢？

G : Well, there's a lot of clutter above the fridge.

格蘭 : 嗯，冰箱上有很多雜物。

If the fire had been any bigger, then it would have spread up there, quickly.

假如那時火勢大一點的話，可能就會因為這些東西而加速蔓延。

P : We had better throw that stuff away, or put it away neatly somewhere.

珮姬 : 那我們最好把那些東西丟掉，或收到其他地方去。

Dialog 對話 2

Grant and Peggy move on to the living room.

格蘭跟珮姬腳步移到客廳。

G : It's funny what you see when you start looking: there's a huge safety hazard in here.

格蘭 : 說來好笑，當你真正檢查起來，就發現有很大的安全漏洞在這兒。

P : I don't see anything wrong.

珮姬 : 我看不出來。

G　　：Take a look at the electrical outlet by the lamp.

格蘭　：你看電燈的插座。

P　　：You're right! There are too many plugs in that outlet.

珮姬　：你說的對！這插座上有好多插頭。

That's a risk for fire.

這樣可能有走火的危險。

G　　：So is the fact that we have our aquarium plugged in nearby.

格蘭　：而且我們把水族箱插頭也插在附近。

If ever there were an earthquake and the water spilled...

萬一哪一天地震，水箱的水灑出來⋯

P　　：Somebody could get a nasty shock.

珮姬　：可能會造成觸電的危險。

 Dialog 對話 3

Peggy and Grant are done looking around their home.

珮姬跟格蘭檢查完他們的家。

G　　：We've got a pretty short list of things to take care of.

格蘭　：其實我們名單上的東西也不多。

But I wonder about our neighbors.
但是我卻擔心我們的鄰居。

P　　：So do I. I know of some people who do silly things like bring space heaters into their bathrooms.

珮姬　：我也是，我聽説有些人還會把暖爐帶進浴室哩。

G　　：And who leave all their junk in stairwells for anyone, including people trying to escape from a fire—to trip over.

格蘭　：還有人會在樓梯間堆放垃圾，這樣火災逃生時會造成跌倒意外。

P　　：Maybe we can try to change people's attitudes about safety.

珮姬　：或許我們可以改變大家對安全的態度。

G　　：What do you have in mind?

格蘭　：你有什麼計畫？

P　　：Well, I'm considering putting up some notices around the building asking everyone to clean up their junk, and pay attention to fire hazards.

珮姬　：這個嘛，我覺得可以張貼公告請各層樓住戶把垃圾處理掉，還有請大家注意用火安全。

Useful Sentences 範例句型

Jeremy asked Keith what else was bothering him about school.

傑洛米問凱斯在學校有什麼不順心的事。

Hearing about her friend's success as a model got Laila thinking about trying out for a fashion show herself.

萊拉聽到朋友成功當了模特兒的消息後，也想著手開辦自己的服裝秀。

After cleaning the bathroom, Mrs. Hill moved on to the kitchen.

整理完浴室，希爾太太又去打掃廚房。

Vocabulary 單字片語

☑ safety	安全
☑ battery	電池
☑ smoke detector	感煙警報器
☑ go off	響起
☑ clutter	雜物
☑ spread	蔓延；擴散
☑ throw something away	丟掉
☑ hazard	危險
☑ electrical	電力的

☑ outlet 插座

☑ plug 插頭；插入

☑ risk （冒）風險

☑ aquarium 水族箱

☑ spill 噴濺出

☑ shock 觸電

☑ space heater 暖爐

MEMO

Keeping Safe on Campus

校園安全

Track-33

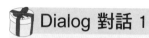
Dialog 對話 1

Grant is telling Megan about his weekend visiting his parents.

格蘭跟梅格談起他週末回家的事情。

G : Except for the fire in the kitchen, it wasn't a very exciting weekend.

格蘭 : 除了廚房的小意外，週末一切都過的很棒。

But I did learn a lot about safety.
而且我的確學到安全的重要性。

M : Are you going to do anything to fire-proof your apartment in Vancouver?

梅格 : 那你要檢查一下你在溫哥華房子的防火措施嗎？

G : I think it's pretty safe already.

格蘭 : 我想那邊已經很安全了。

What I'm worried about is burglaries.
我擔心的是闖空門問題。

M : Is that a problem in your neighborhood?

梅格 : 你住的地區有這個問題？

G : Yes. Several people in my building have had break-ins in recent months.

格蘭 : 對啊，這幾個月有幾個人家裡都被小偷光顧了。

M : Then you should be extra careful to keep your doors locked tight!

梅格 : 那你更要小心，隨時把門窗鎖好囉。

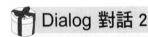 Dialog 對話 2

Grant and Megan continue their discussion.
格蘭跟梅格繼續討論。

G : I guess you're lucky that you live on campus.

格蘭 : 我想或許還是跟你一樣住校好吧。

While you have to worry about noisy roommates and dirty bathrooms, you have peace of mind.

雖然要擔心室友很吵，或是浴室很髒，但至少內心還滿有安全感的。

M : How's that?

梅格 : 怎麼說？

G : Because you know you're perfectly safe.

格蘭 : 因為你可以確定環境是很安全的。

No one will break into your room.
沒有人會闖進你的房間。

M　　：Maybe not, but campus is pretty big, and some areas are secluded.

梅格　：或許不會，不過校園很大，還是有些幽僻的地方不安全。

There are other things to worry about.

總有其他危險要擔心。

G　　：I guess it might be kind of scary to walk around there at night if you're alone.

格蘭　：我想晚上單獨走在這兒還是滿可怕的吧。

M　　：That's why there's the Safe-walk program.

梅格　：這也是為什麼要實施校園「行走安全」措施啊。

 Dialog 對話 3

Grant has never heard of Safe-walk and asks Megan to tell him more about it.

格蘭從沒聽過「行走安全」這東西，所以他跟梅格多討教一些。

M　　：It's pretty straight forward.

梅格　：其實很簡單。

The program ensures that students who have to walk from one part of campus to another after dark are safe.

這是可以確保學生夜行校園的安全措施。

G　　：Can you give me an example?

格蘭　：可以舉個例嗎？

M　　：Sure.

梅格　：當然。

Let's say that I have to spend the evening studying in the library, but it's late when I'm done.

假設我在圖書館唸書到很晚，當我要出來時天已很暗了。

I can go to the Safe-walk kiosk, and a pair of student volunteers will walk me to my car.

我就可以到「行走安全」亭，就會有幾個學生義工陪我走到我的車子那兒去。

G　　：Really? That's great!

格蘭　：真的？這太棒了！

M　　：I think so, too.

梅格　：我也這麼覺得。

That's why next semester, when I'm not so busy, I'm going to volunteer to be one of the walkers.

因為這樣，我也將加入自願糾察隊的行列。

G　　：That's the spirit!

格蘭　：精神可嘉喔！

Useful Sentences 範例句型

Except for a quarter, I don't have any money at all!

我身上只剩一個銅板了！

Gillian kept her diary locked tight in case her sister tried to read it.

吉蓮把自己的日記鎖好以免被妹妹偷看。

Having a lot of money in the bank gave Farrah peace of mind.

銀行存款寬裕使法拉內心感到有保障。

The instructions for putting the bookshelf together were straightforward, so Tim finished the job quickly.

拼裝書櫃的說明很簡單，因此提姆很快就完成工作。

Vocabulary 單字片語

☑ fireproof	防火措施
☑ burglary	竊盜；闖空門
☑ break in	闖入
☑ recent	最近的
☑ secluded	幽僻的
☑ ensure	確保
☑ kiosk	亭子
☑ volunteer	自願者

Speeding Ticket
超速罰單

🔘 Track-34

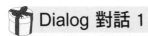 Dialog 對話 1

Helen is driving to Grant's apartment in her father's car. Suddenly, she notices a police siren and flashing lights. She pulls over.

海倫正開著爸爸的車去找格蘭。突然她聽到一陣警笛聲，警車還亮起了警燈，因此她將車子靠邊停下。

H   : Yes, officer?

海倫   : 警察先生，有什麼問題嗎？

O   : Please turn your engine off, Miss.

警察   : 小姐，麻煩你將車子熄火。

        License and registration, please.

        請給我你的駕照、行照。

H   : Here you are.

海倫   : 好的。

O   : Do you know how fast you were going back there?

警察   : 你知道你剛才的車速多少嗎？

H   : Umm…no, actually, I don't remember.

海倫   : 呃…不知道，我忘記了。

O : You were driving at seventy-five kilometers an hour.

警察 : 你已經開到時速七十五公里了。

That's well over the speed limit.

這已經超過速限了。

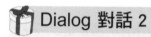 Dialog 對話 2

The officer goes to his car to write a ticket and comes back to talk to Helen.

警察走回警車，開了單子後，再回來跟海倫說話。

H : So, am I going to get a ticket?

海倫 : 嗯，我要被開單嗎？

O : Yes. You can send the payment in by mail.

警察 : 沒錯，你可以用郵政劃撥繳罰款。

H : Ouch. This is a big fine.

海倫 : 天啊，罰這麼重。

O : Perhaps next time you'll be more careful about obeying the speed limits.

警察 : 這樣你下次應該會更注意要遵守速限。

H : Yes, sir.

海倫 : 是的，警官。

O : That's all, Miss. You may go.

警察 : 就這樣小姐，你可以走了。

🎁 Dialog 對話 3

Helen is at Grant's place.
海倫在格蘭家。

G　： I'm sorry to hear you got a ticket.
格蘭　： 聽到你被開單，真讓人難過。

H　： So am I! I don't know what I'm going to do!
海倫　： 我也是！我真不知道該怎麼辦！

G　： Well, if you're short of cash, don't worry!
格蘭　： 嗯，如果你錢不夠，不用擔心！

　　　I can try to help you out...
　　　我可以借你⋯

H　： It's not the money I'm worried about.
海倫　： 我不是擔心錢的事。

　　　It's the fact that I took my dad's car without permission.
　　　其實我當初沒問我爸就把他的車開出來。

G　： And now he'll find out that you were in Vancouver with it.
格蘭　： 這下他就知道你把車子開到溫哥華來了。

H　： Yes. When he finds out he's going to kill me.
海倫　： 對啊，等他發現，他會殺了我的。

185

Useful Sentences 範例句型

On the highway, most cars go around 100 kilometers per hour!

高速公路上的車幾乎都開到時速一百！

Kim got a second job because she was well over her budget for the year.

金又兼了第二份工作，因為她已經透支一年了。

Evan was short of cash so he had to borrow some money from his friend.

伊文因為缺錢，所以得開口跟朋友借錢。

Susan was so angry at her brother she wanted to kill him!

蘇珊氣她兄弟氣到真想宰了他！

Vocabulary 單字片語

☑ siren	警鈴
☑ flashing	閃光燈
☑ engine	引擎
☑ license	駕照
☑ registration	行照
☑ speed limit	速限
☑ ticket	罰單
☑ ouch	噢！
☑ fine	罰款
☑ obey	遵守
☑ permission	允許

Gone in Sixty Seconds

一眨眼就不見了

 Track-35

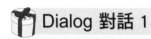 Dialog 對話 1

After visiting Grant, Helen is feeling a little bit better. Grant walks her downstairs to the street.

拜訪完格蘭，海倫心情好多了。格蘭陪她下樓到街上。

G　　：Where did you park, Helen?
格蘭　：海倫，你車停哪？

H　　：Right here, I think. But maybe on the next block.
海倫　：應該就在這，不過有可能停在下一條巷子裡。

G　　：Alright, let's walk!
格蘭　：好，我們走吧！

H　　：I don't see it. Maybe it's around the corner.
海倫　：我沒看到，或許在轉角那邊。

G　　：No Honda Accords there, either.
格蘭　：轉角沒有半台本田車啊。

　　　Did you park on a red line?
　　　你停紅線嗎？

H   : Gosh, I don't think so!
海倫   : 我的天，應該不會吧！

But I could have...I guess we had better call the car impound lot.
可是有可能⋯我看我們最好打個電話給拖吊管制中心。

I could have been towed.
可能被吊走了。

 Dialog 對話 2

Grant is calling the city impound lot. He is speaking to a clerk there on the phone.
格蘭打電話到拖吊處。他在跟一個辦事員說話。

G   : Pardon me.
格蘭   : 不好意思。

I need to know if you've impounded a car at your lot within the last three hours?
我想請問一下，你們在這三小時內有拖吊扣押任何車子嗎？

C   : Where would it have been towed from?
辦事員 : 你的車是在哪被拖走的？

G   : Fifth Avenue.
格蘭   : 第五大道。

C : What make and model, sir?

辦事員 : 哪種車型？

G : A Honda Accord.

格蘭 : 本田。

C : I'm sorry, sir, but there's no record of a car matching that description on our lot.

辦事員 : 很抱歉，我們這邊沒有你說的那種車喔。

 Dialog 對話 3

Grant tells Helen the bad news.
格蘭跟海倫說結果。

H : Are you sure?

海倫 : 你確定？

G : Yes. The car's not there, which means only one thing…

格蘭 : 對，車子沒被拖走，那就只有一種可能了…

H : I can't bring myself to say it!

海倫 : 我不敢說！

G : The car has been stolen.

格蘭 : 車子被偷了。

H : I can't believe my rotten luck!

海倫 : 我真不敢相信我會倒楣到這種地步！

G　　　: Don't cry, Helen.

格蘭　: 別哭。

I'll go with you to the police department and help you make your report.

我陪你去警局報失竊，他們做筆錄時我會幫你的。

Useful Sentences 範例句型

It only took Paul a few minutes to get to school because it was just around the corner from his house.

保羅只要花幾分鐘就可以到學校，因為他家離學校很近。

To get the clerk's attention, James said "Pardon me!"

為了引起店員注意，詹姆斯拿「不好意思！」當開場白。

Nobody wanted to tell Janine the bad news, but finally I did.

沒人敢跟珍妮說這件壞消息，最後只好由我說了。

The clouds in the sky can only mean one thing: Rain!

天空烏雲密佈，只有一種可能：要下雨了！

Vocabulary 單字片語

☑ block 街；巷

☑ gosh 天啊！

☑ impound 扣押；保管

☑ tow 拖吊

☑ make 製廠

☑ model 款型

☑ match 符合

☑ description 描述

☑ lot 場地

☑ rotten 爛透了的

☑ record 記錄

MEMO

....

....

....

....

....

....

....

....

Asking for Directions

問路

 Dialog 對話 1

Grant and Helen are unsure of where the police department is, so Grant goes into a store and asks a clerk.

格蘭跟海倫都不確定警局在哪，所以格蘭到一家商店去問店員。

G : Excuse me. Can you tell me where the nearest police station is?

格蘭 : 不好意思，請問你知道這附近哪裡有警察局嗎？

C : Sure. It's on Eighth Street.

服務員 : 當然，第八街就有。

G : I'm sorry, but I've only lived in this neighborhood for a few months.

格蘭 : 對不起，我才剛搬來幾個月而已。

I'm not sure where that is.
我不太清楚第八街在哪。

C : It's not far from here.

服務員 : 離這不遠。

When you leave the store, turn left.
你出了店門後，左轉。

Walk for three blocks, and turn left again at the first alley.
走過三個路口後，第一個巷子左轉。

G : Yes?
格蘭 : 然後？

C : Walk until the first intersection.
服務員 : 繼續走，直到第一個十字路口。

The police station will be across the street!
警察局就在對面！

 Dialog **對話** 2

Helen and Grant are leaving the police station.
海倫跟格蘭離開警局。

H : I guess I'll be taking the bus home.
海倫 : 看來我得搭公車回家。

G : I wish I had a car so that I could drive you.
格蘭 : 真希望我有車可以載你回家。

H : That's OK.
海倫 : 沒關係。

193

I'm not worried about the bus ride, but I am worried about facing my dad when I get in the door.

坐公車不是問題，我怕的是回家後就要面對我爸。

G : That's going to be tough.

格蘭 : 這的確是個難題。

If you need any moral support, you know you can call me anytime.

假如你需要任何精神支持，隨時都可以打電話給我。

H : I'm sure I'll be taking you up on that offer.

海倫 : 我相信會派上用場的。

You've been so helpful today, Grant. I really appreciate it.

你已經幫我很大的忙了，格蘭，真的很感謝。

G : No worries! That's what boyfriends are for!

格蘭 : 小意思！這是男朋友應該做的！

 Dialog 對話 3

Helen and Grant are looking for the bus stop.

海倫跟格蘭在找公車站牌。

H : If we don't find the bus stop soon, I'll likely miss the last bus back.

海倫 : 再不找到公車站，我就趕不上最後一班車了。

G : You can spend the night at my place if you need to.

格蘭 : 真不行的話，你可以在我家過夜。

H : Then my dad will have to kill me twice!

海倫 : 那我爸會殺我兩次！

No, I've got to find the bus stop, pronto.
不行，我一定要馬上找到公車站。

I'm going to ask that man. Excuse me, sir.
我去問那個人。先生，不好意思。

M : Yes?

陌生人 : 什麼事？

G : Do you know where I can catch the bus to White Rock?

格蘭 : 請問你知道哪裡有去白石鎮的公車嗎？

M : Yes. The bus stop is on Front Road.

陌生人 : 知道，主線道那邊就有個站牌。

Take a right at the stop sign and walk for two blocks. You can't miss it!
紅綠燈那邊右轉，再走過二個路口。你就會看到了！

Useful Sentences 範例句型

Henry didn't want to face his friends after they found out that he had said bad things about them.

亨利沒臉見他的朋友，因為他在背後說他們壞話，被他們知道了。

Josh gave his brother moral support and listened to him when he broke up with his girlfriend.

當喬許的哥哥跟女朋友分手時，喬許除了給他精神支持外，還扮演傾聽者的角色。

After taking Doug up on his offer to teach me math, my grades have gotten much better!

讓道格教我數學後，我的成績就進步很多了！

As soon as Wendy walked in the door, the phone rang.

溫蒂才一走進家門，電話就響了。

Vocabulary 單字片語

☑	directions	方向
☑	unsure	不確定的
☑	station	車站
☑	turn	轉彎
☑	alley	巷道
☑	intersection	十字路口
☑	across	穿過
☑	pronto	馬上；立刻

Unit 7

Losing a Wallet
遺失皮包

 Track-37

 Dialog 對話 1

Helen is about to get off the bus in White Rock. As she reaches for her wallet to pay for her fare, her face goes white.

海倫正要下公車。當她伸手拿錢包時,她臉色發白。

D　　: That'll be three dollars, Miss.
駕駛　: 小姐,車資三塊。

H　　: Just a second, I can't find my wallet...
海倫　: 等等,我找不到錢包…

D　　: Could you please stand to the side, then, so that other passengers can alight?
駕駛　: 那你先站到旁邊去,讓其他乘客先下車好嗎?

H　　: Sorry…Where is it?
海倫　: 對不起…到哪去了?

D　　: Do you have the fare, Miss?
駕駛　: 小姐,你到底有沒有錢啊?

H　　: No, I'm sorry. I don't. I think I've lost my wallet!
海倫　: 沒有,對不起,我的錢包好像掉了。

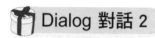 Dialog 對話 2

A kind stranger approaches Helen.
一位好心的陌生人走向海倫。

S   : You've lost your wallet?
陌生人 ： 你的錢包掉了嗎？

H   : Yes. I can't seem to find it.
海倫   ： 對，我實在找不到。

S   : How much money do you need?
陌生人 ： 你需要多少錢？

H   : Three dollars.
海倫   ： 三塊錢。

S   : Here you go.
陌生人 ： 來，給你。

H   : You're so kind! Thank you very much.
海倫   ： 你真是太好心了！多謝你！

        Can I have your phone number so that I can pay you back?
        你可以留個電話給我，好讓我把錢還清嗎？

S   : That's alright. It's only three dollars.
陌生人 ： 不用還了，才三塊錢而已。

I hope someone will do the same for my daughter if she ever needs help.

假如我女兒遇到這種狀況時，我希望也有人可以這樣幫她。

🎁 Dialog 對話 3

As she walks home, Helen calls Grant and tells him what happened.

當海倫走回家時，她打電話給格蘭，訴說剛發生的事。

G : Helen, you are having the worst string of luck.

格蘭 : 海倫，你真是倒楣到極點了。

H : Hopefully it's over now.

海倫 : 希望楣運已經結束了。

You know what they say: "Bad luck comes in threes."

不是有句話說「事不過三」嗎？

G : That's true.

格蘭 : 是啊。

Listen, you probably shouldn't be talking with me on the phone right now, though.

不過，現在不是跟我講電話的時候。

H : What kind of boyfriend are you! You said to call anytime if I needed your help!

海倫 : 你算什麼男朋友啊！你還說有需要我都可以打給你！

G : I just mean you should probably call your credit card company and have them suspend your line of credit.

格蘭 : 我的意思是，你應該先打電話到信用卡公司掛失才對。

H : Good idea.

海倫 : 沒錯。

G : And while you do that, I'll retrace our steps today.

格蘭 : 你去處理你的卡，我一邊沿著我們今天走過的路找找看。

Who knows? Your luck might change for the better, and I might find your wallet.

誰知道，風水輪流轉，說不定我待會就找到你的錢包了。

Useful Sentences 範例句型

Brenda's face went white when she heard that she'd failed the test.

布蘭達一聽到考試考壞的消息，臉色馬上蒼白。

The teacher asked her students to stand to the side of the path while the other class passed by.

老師要學生們靠邊站，好讓其他班的學生先過。

Richard had a great string of luck: first, he got into the university he applied for, and then he won a scholarship!

理察運氣實在很好，先是被申請的學校錄用，後來又得到了獎學金！

Making a change for the better, Chris decided to stop smoking.

為了有番新氣象，克里斯決定戒煙。

Vocabulary 單字片語

☑	reach for something	伸向
☑	alight	通過
☑	fare	車錢
☑	wallet	皮包
☑	suspend	掛失
☑	line of credit	信用卡交易
☑	retrace	尋找
☑	steps	腳步；蹤跡

Unit 8

Lending a Helping Hand

伸出援手

 Track-38

 Dialog 對話 1

One week later, things in Helen's house have calmed down. The family's car has been recovered, and Helen's father is less angry. Helen is in her bedroom talking to her brother, Doug.

一個禮拜後，海倫家的風波總算稍微平息了。家裡的車找到了，海倫的爸爸也氣消了。海倫在房裡跟哥哥道格說話。

D　　: You've had a pretty bad week!

駕駛　: 你這禮拜真的很慘！

　　　But things are taking a turn for the better now.

　　　不過現在應該開始轉運了吧。

H　　: Lucky for me!

海倫　: 那就好！

　　　But you know, as bad as everything has been, some nice things have happened, too.

　　　不過說真的，雖然很多倒楣事發生，但至少也有一些好事情。

202

D　　　: Like Dad not kicking you out of the house?!

駕駛　: 你是說，至少老爸沒把你趕出家門嗎 ?!

H　　　: Like the stranger who helped me out on the bus.

海倫　: 我是說，那個在車上借我錢的陌生人。

D　　　: You mean the guy who gave you a measly three dollars?

駕駛　: 你是說那個給你三塊錢的人？

H　　　: It was the gesture that mattered.

海倫　: 是他的心意讓人感動。

He was just a stranger, but his kindness made a difference.

他只是個陌生人，但他的善舉卻改變了一切。

And I'll do something kind in return, when I get the chance.

因此有機會我一定要做點善事以示感恩。

Dialog 對話 2

Helen is walking to the bus stop when she witnesses a car accident. She runs over to the car that looks more badly damaged and speaks to the driver.

當海倫走到公車站時，她目睹了一個車禍。她趕緊跑向嚴重損壞的汽車，試圖跟駕駛說話。

H	:	Are you alright?
海倫	:	你還好嗎？

D	:	Yes, I think so.
駕駛	:	應該還好。

But I think my arm might be broken.
但是我的手可能骨折了。

H	:	Let me try to help you out of your car.
海倫	:	讓我扶你出來。

D	:	Thank you.
駕駛	:	謝謝。

But first, could you please take some pictures of the scene with my camera?
你可以先幫我把車禍情況，用我的相機照下來嗎？

H	:	Sure. It's important to have a record of these events.
海倫	:	當然，留下存證紀錄是很重要的。

D	:	It is. I'm sorry I forgot to ask you, are you in a hurry today?
駕駛	:	沒錯，不好意思，我剛忘了問，你有在趕時間嗎？

If not, I'd appreciate it if you'd stay and speak to the police.
假如沒有，我希望你可以留下來跟警方說明。

You can tell them what you saw.
你可以跟他們說你目擊到的情況。

H　　　: No problem, but first, the pictures.

海倫　　: 沒問題，不過我們先拍照吧。

 Dialog 對話 3

Helen has just finished talking to the police.
She's continues on her way to the bus stop
when she crosses paths with a beggar.

海倫跟警察說完話後，繼續走向車站。她在路上遇到一個乞
丐。

B　　　: Spare any change?

乞丐　　: 有零錢嗎？

H　　　: Pardon me?

海倫　　: 什麼？

B　　　: I'm hungry and I need some money to buy
　　　　 something to eat.

乞丐　　: 我很餓，我想要一點錢買東西吃。

H　　　: Here's two dollars. I hope it helps.

海倫　　: 這是二塊錢，希望夠你用。

B　　　: Thank you, Miss.

乞丐　　: 小姐，謝謝你。

H　　　: You're welcome. Take care of yourself.

海倫　　: 不客氣，自己保重。

Useful Sentences 範例句型

It had been years since I've crossed paths with any of my old classmates.

> 我已經有好幾年沒遇到老同學了。

Tom was kicked out of university after he had been found cheating on a test.

> 湯姆因為考試作弊，被踢出大學校門。

Studying every night really made a difference in Greta's grades.

> 每晚用功讀書讓葛瑞塔的成績大有改觀。

Polly hoped she'd get the chance to act in the town play this year.

> 寶莉希望今年她可以在縣市公演中得到演出機會。

Vocabulary 單字片語

☑	calm down	冷靜下來
☑	recover	發現
☑	measly	僅；只
☑	gesture	手勢；動作
☑	witness	目擊
☑	damage	損傷
☑	camera	照相機
☑	beggar	乞丐
☑	spare	多的
☑	change	零錢

At the Hospital
在醫院

Track-39

 Dialog 對話 1

Back on campus, Megan and Kurt are playing intramural volleyball. Megan jumps up to block a shot, but slips when she lands and falls on the ground.

回到校園，梅格跟科特在打排球。梅格跳起來擋球，落地時卻滑倒了。

M　　：Oww! My arm!

梅格　：噢！我的手！

K　　：Meg! Are you alright? Is it broken?

科特　：梅格！你沒事吧？有骨折嗎？

M　　：I don't know, maybe.

梅格　：不知道，有可能。

K　　：Can you move your hand and your wrist, like this?

科特　：你可以把手腕這樣動嗎？

M　　：Uh-huh…oww!

梅格　：呃…噢！

K : I think it's time for a little trip to the Emergency Room.

科特 ： 看來我們得掛急診了。

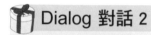 Dialog 對話 2

Megan goes to the check-in desk and speaks to a receptionist.

梅格到掛號台跟辦事人員說話。

M : Is there a doctor available to see me?

梅格 ： 有醫生可以幫我看診嗎？

R : What's the problem?

辦事員 ： 有什麼問題嗎？

M : I fell down and hurt my arm playing volleyball.

梅格 ： 我打排球時摔倒，手臂受傷了。

R : I see. Doctor Hsu will be available soon.

辦事員 ： 好，蘇醫師很快就過來了。

　　　　　Can you fill out this form?

　　　　　請你填一下這份表格好嗎？

M : Probably not—I usually write with my right hand, but it hurts.

梅格 ： 可能不行，我是右撇子，現在又剛好右手受傷。

　　　　　Can my friend fill it out for me?

　　　　　可以叫我朋友幫我寫嗎？

R : Certainly. May I see your health insurance card, please.

辦事員 : 當然，可以給我看一下你的健保卡嗎？

Thank you. You can take a seat in the waiting area, and go to the doctor's office when your number is called.

謝謝，請你先在等候區稍待，叫到你的號碼時，你就可以進去看醫生了。

 Dialog 對話 3

Megan is sitting in the doctor's office. He has just finished examining her arm.

梅格在診療室裡。醫生剛檢查完她的手。

M : Will I need a cast?

梅格 : 我要上石膏嗎？

D : Possibly.

醫生 : 可能。

I need to take an x-ray to be sure, but it seems that your arm is fractured.

看起來似乎有骨折，我要照張 X 光才能確定。

M : How long will I need to wear it?

梅格 : 我要裹石膏裹多久？

D : For about four weeks.

醫生 : 大概四個禮拜。

That's the time it will take for the bone to heal.

通常要這麼久的時間，骨頭才有辦法癒合。

M : Is there anything you can do for the pain? It hurts a lot!

梅格 : 那你可以幫我止痛嗎？這真的很痛！

D : Yes. I'll prescribe some mild painkillers.

醫生 : 我可以幫你上一些止痛軟膏。

They should make you more comfortable.

這樣你應該就會好一點了。

Now if you'll follow me, we can take that x-ray of your arm.

你現在跟我來，我們去照張 X 光片。

Useful Sentences 範例句型

The crowd cheered when Yao Ming blocked a shot during the basketball game.

當姚明蓋對方火鍋時，全場觀眾一片歡呼。

The teacher told the students to be quiet and take their seats.

老師要學生安靜地找位子坐下。

In the time that it took for Paula to clean her room, her sister had not only cleaned her room, but done the shopping and laundry too

寶拉花在整理房間的時間，她妹不但可以把房間整理好，東西都買好了，連衣服都洗好了。

The stray dog followed Bernard all the way home.

那隻流浪狗一路跟著貝納到家。

Vocabulary 單字片語

☑ block		阻擋
☑ slip		滑倒
☑ land		落地
☑ wrist		手腕
☑ Emergency Room		急診室
☑ check in		掛號
☑ receptionist		辦事接待員
☑ fill out		填好
☑ health insurance card		健保卡
☑ waiting area		等候區
☑ examine		檢查
☑ cast		石膏
☑ x-ray		X 光
☑ fracture		骨折
☑ prescribe		開處方

All's Well that Ends Well

喜劇收場

 Dialog 對話 1

It's the end of the semester, and to celebrate, Grant is throwing a party. All of his friends from school are there.

為了慶祝學期即將結束，格蘭辦了個派對。所有學校的朋友都在場。

G : Hey, Megan! I've been wondering how you're doing.

格蘭 : 嘿，梅格！我還在想說你最近怎麼樣了。

I haven't seen you since your accident.
自從你受傷後，我就沒再看到你了。

M : I'm great!

梅格 : 我很好！

My doctor says my arm is healing well and he'll take my cast off next week.
醫生說我的手復原很快，下禮拜就可以拆石膏了。

G : That's great news!
真是大好的消息！

M : Yes, and no.

梅格 : 有好有壞。

I'm happy the cast is coming off because it's been inconvenient to shower. I have to be careful not to get it wet.

可以拆石膏是不錯，因為包著石膏洗澡時，我都得小心不能弄濕。

G : I can understand that.

格蘭 : 我了解。

M : However, with final exams coming, having my arm in a cast would be a good excuse not to write them!

梅格 : 可是期末考要到了，包著石膏，我才有理由不寫考卷！

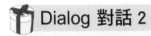 Dialog 對話 2

Grant goes to mingle with his other guests.

格蘭去跟其他客人聊天。

G : Are you having a good time, Celia?

格蘭 : 莎莉亞，你玩的盡興嗎？

C : You bet!

莎莉亞 : 當然！

Although, I was hoping this would be a dinner party.

其實我當初比較希望這是個晚餐聚會。

G : I've hung up my apron I'm afraid.

格蘭 : 我已經封廚，不做菜了。

I'm a danger to myself and to others.

因為我怕我會給大家帶來危險。

C : Are you referring to the fire you started?!

莎莉亞 : 你是說之前廚房起火的事嗎？！

G : Yes. Did Helen tell you about it?

格蘭 : 對啊，海倫跟你說的？

C : She did.

莎莉亞 : 對。

And about how much she misses your cooking now that you're afraid of causing a six-alarm blaze!

她也跟我說，她很想念你的拿手好菜，可是你卻擔心引發六級大火災。

 Dialog 對話 3

Grant finds Helen in the kitchen putting snacks on plates.

格蘭看到海倫在廚房將點心裝盤。

G : There you are! Have you been hiding out in here all night?

格蘭 : 你在這兒啊！你打算整晚都躲在這兒嗎？

H	: Nope, I've mixed and mingled.
海倫	: 沒有啊，我已經跟大夥兒打過照面了。

G	: Are you having a good time?
格蘭	: 你玩的愉快嗎？

H	: I am.
海倫	: 愉快啊。

G	: Good. It's about time a smile returned to your face.
格蘭	: 太好了，你也該再度展開笑顏了。

H	: Thanks. I feel the same way.
海倫	: 謝謝，我也這麼覺得呢。

Useful Sentences 範例句型

Fred thought that complaining of a headache would be a good excuse to stay at home instead of going to the movies with some people he didn't really like.

佛瑞德認為，拿頭痛當藉口待在家裡，總比跟一群他不喜歡的人去看電影好的多。

The boy who ran around the playground with a pair of scissors in his hands was a danger to himself and to others.

在遊樂場裡拿著剪刀到處跑的小男孩，對自己或他人都是一種安全上的威脅。

The smile returned to the sad girl's face when her boyfriend gave her a dozen roses.

當男友獻上一束玫瑰時，傷心的女孩終於再展笑顏。

Harris nodded his head because he felt the same way as Dorothy.

哈瑞斯點頭，因為他跟朵瑞絲有同樣的感受。

Vocabulary 單字片語

☑ throw a party	舉辦派對
☑ come off	拿掉
☑ inconvenient	不便
☑ shower	沖澡
☑ mingle	融入
☑ hang up one's apron	不下廚了
☑ refer	提到
☑ a six-alarm blaze	大火災

Chapter 5

That's Entertainment

那才是娛樂

When it's the weekend, how do you like to relax? When the students at Vancouver University put away their books to have some fun, they do many different things. Going to catch a movie is a popular choice, as is hanging out with friends drinking tea at a restaurant. Whatever they do, though, they have one thing in common: they know it's important to relax so that they don't burn out.

週末時，你會從事什麼休閒活動？當溫哥華大學的學生們放下書本，去放鬆充電時，他們的花樣可多了。最常見的休閒活動是看電影，或是三五好友一起到餐廳喝茶聊天。然而，不論從事什麼休閒活動，他們都有一個共通觀念，那就是「休息是為了走更長遠的路」。

Unit 1

At the Movies
看電影

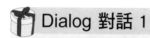

Dialog 對話 1

Grant calls Megan and asks her if she's free to see a movie.

格蘭打電話問給梅格是問她是否有空可以去看場電影。

M : What do you have in mind?
梅格 : 你有什麼計畫嗎？

G : I wanted to see the new Jet Li flick.
格蘭 : 我想去看李連杰的新片。

M : An action movie? How about a comedy?
梅格 : 動作片啊？看喜劇片好不好？

G : Alright, as long as it's not romantic.
格蘭 : 可以！只要不是愛情片就好了。

M : I can live with that. How about the latest Jim Carrey film?
梅格 : 沒問題。那麼看金凱瑞的新片如何？

G   : Sorry, but I saw that one last weekend with Helen.

格蘭 : 不好意思，那部片我上禮拜和已經和海倫一起看過了。

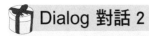 Dialog 對話 2

Grant and Megan are still trying to figure our which movie to see.

格蘭和梅格還在考慮要看哪部片。

G   : How about a drama? There's a new version of Shakespeare's Hamlet out.

格蘭 : 戲劇片呢？有一個新改拍的「哈姆雷特」正在上映。

M   : Hmm...I saw the trailer for that a while ago, and it didn't look too bad. Alright, let's see that one.

梅格 : 嗯…我之前有看過它的預告片，看起來還不錯。好吧！我們看這部吧！

G   : Great. All we need to know is the"when"and the"where".

格蘭 : 太好了，現在我們只要確定時間跟地點就好了。

M   : Can you look up the movie listings on your computer?

梅格 : 你可以在你的電腦上查電影時刻表嗎？

G : I can't. My ADSL connection is down.

格蘭 ：不行啊。我的 ADSL 網路連線已經斷了。

M : Never mind. I have today's paper. I can check out what's playing in the Entertainment section.

梅格 ：沒關係，我有今天的報紙，我可以在娛樂版上查一下正在上映的電影。

 Dialog 對話 3

Megan has opened the paper and is looking at the movie listings.
梅格打開了今天的報紙，查看電影時刻表。

M : Let's see...Hamlet...It's playing at Oak Center and at Silver City.

梅格 ：讓我看看…「哈姆雷特」…在橡木影城和銀色世界上映。

G : Any location is fine by me. The time is more important.

格蘭 ：我哪裡都可以，看的時間比較重要。

M : Do you want to see an early show, or a late one?

梅格 ：你想要看早場還是晚一點的？

G : An early one. Tomorrow I have to wake up early to meet Helen. We have a tennis match.

格蘭 ：早場。明天我得找起去見海倫，我們有一個網球比賽。

M   : OK. There's a seven fifteen show at Oak Center.

梅格 ：好，在橡木影城七點十五分有一場。

G   : Sounds Great! I'll meet you there!

格蘭 ：聽起來不錯！那我們就約在那裡！

Useful Sentences 範例句型

Debra decided she could live with her ugly old car after finding out how expensive a new one would be.

黛柏拉發現一台新車有多貴之後，決定繼續忍受她醜醜的老爺車。

The concert starts playing at nine o'clock.

音樂會在九點開始演出。

Rick didn't know how to spell the word so he looked it up in the dictionary.

瑞奇不知道如何拼那個字，因此他查了字典。

When Oliver apologized for being late, Penny just said "Never mind."

當奧立佛為了遲到而道歉時，潘妮只說了「沒關係」。

Vocabulary 單字片語

☑	be free to do something	有空做什麼
☑	flick	電影
☑	action movie	動作電影
☑	comedy	喜劇電影
☑	romantic	愛情電影
☑	latest	最新的
☑	figure out	決定
☑	drama	戲劇
☑	version	版本
☑	be out	上映
☑	trailer	預告片
☑	ADSL connection	ADSL 網路連線
☑	entertainment	娛樂
☑	section	版面
☑	tennis	網球

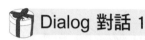 Dialog 對話 1

Megan and Grant meet at Oak Center.
梅格和格蘭在橡木影城碰面。

G : Man, this line is long!

格蘭 ：唉，排隊排得很長。

M : It's too bad we didn't think to order our tickets over the telephone.

梅格 ：我們當初怎麼沒想到要用電話訂票。

G : Come again?

格蘭 ：你說什麼？

M : You can order tickets to see the movie of your choice over the phone, provided you have a credit card.

格 ：只要有信用卡，你就可以直接透過電話預定你要的電影票。

G : What a cool idea! It would certainly beat standing in line.

格蘭 ：這主意真酷！一定比在這裡排隊來得好。

M : It would. This time, I guess we'll just have to bite the bullet.

梅格 : 沒錯，事到如今我們只好忍耐了。

 Dialog 對話 2

After fifteen minutes, Grant and Megan are at the front of the line.

經過十五分鐘後，終於輪到格蘭和梅格。

C : Next!

售票員：下一位！

G : Hi! Two tickets for "Hamlet", please.

格蘭 : 嗨！請給我兩張「哈姆雷特」的票。

C : Which show?

售票員：哪一場？

G : The early show.

格蘭 : 早場。

C : Hmm...all that we have left are seats in the first three rows. Is that OK?

售票員：嗯…我們只剩下前三排的位子了，可以嗎？

G : Yep, no problem.

格蘭 : 好，可以。

C : That'll be six dollars, please!

售票員：總共是六塊錢！

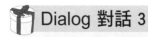 Dialog 對話 3

Grant and Megan are sitting in row three while the opening credits are rolling.
當片頭字幕開始時，格蘭和梅格正坐進第三排裡。

M : If I had have known that we'd be sitting in the third row, I would have insisted on seeing a later showing.

梅格 : 早知道我們會坐在第三排，我就會堅持看晚一點的場次。

G : Sorry! But it's not so bad—at least there's nobody tall sitting in front of you!

格蘭 : 對不起！但是，至少不會有高個子坐你前面！

M : There's nobody sitting in front of me, period!

梅格 : 前面根本不會有人坐，完畢！

G : Shh! The show's about to start!

格蘭 : 噓！電影要開始了！

M : Did you remember to turn off your cell phone?

梅格 : 你有把手機關機嗎？

G : Yes! Now, shh!

格蘭 : 有啦，噓！

Useful Sentences 範例句型

Andy knew that working in an office would beat having to do physical labor.

安迪認為坐辦公室應該比出賣勞力的工作好一點。

John didn't have much money. But he had to bite the bullet and pay a thousand dollars to repair his car.

約翰不是很有錢，但是他還是得忍痛付出一千多元，請人幫他修理車子。

Jenny didn't hear what Jack said on the phone, so she said "Come again?"

珍妮並沒有聽到傑克在電話裡說的話，所以她說：「什麼？」

Danny said there was no way he'd wear a dress, period

丹尼說要他穿女洋裝是不可能的事，就這樣。

Vocabulary 單字片語

☑ row	一行；排
☑ credits	片頭字幕
☑ roll	播放
☑ insist	堅持

Renting a Video

租錄影帶

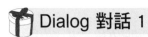

Dialog 對話 1

Celia and Kurt are trying to figure out how to spend their Friday night.

莎莉亞和科特正在思考如何度過星期五晚上。

K : Let's go to a nightclub.

科特 : 我們去夜店。

C : Nah. Nightclubs are only fun if a lot of your friends are interested in going.

莎莉亞 : 不要，夜店只有跟一大票朋友去才好玩。

K : For some reason all of our friends are busy tonight.

科特 : 可是偏偏這次大家好像都沒空。

C : So, it's just you and me, baby!

莎莉亞 : 所以，就只剩你和我啦，寶貝！

K : Want to catch a flick? The new Schwarzenegger movie is opening...

科特 : 看場電影怎樣？史瓦茲辛格的新電影正開始上映…。

C : Please! By now all the movies have been sold out. We'd only catch a midnight showing, if we

---

were lucky.

莎莉亞 ： 拜託，現在所有的電影票都已經賣完了。運氣好的話頂多也只能看午夜場。

 Dialog 對話 2

Kurt and Celia are still trying to figure out what to do for fun.
科特和莎莉亞還在考慮要做什麼好玩的事。

C ： Well, if we can't go see a movie, then maybe we should rent a video.

莎莉亞 ： 嗯！如果我們不能去看電影，那麼也許我們可以去租個錄影帶。

K ： That's a good idea. But we may still run into the same problem …

科特 ： 好主意，但是我們可能還是會遇到同樣的問題。

C ： … that the video store is all out of new releases? That's OK.

莎莉亞 ： …你是說新片都沒了？沒關係啊。

K ： You mean you're willing to watch something you've seen before?

科特 ： 你還想看已經看過的片子？

C ： Not exactly. I'm willing to rent a classic.

莎莉亞 ： 也不是，租一部經典老片也不錯啊。

K   : I see. But only as a last resort!

科特   : 我明白了，不過這是情非得已的時候喔！

 Dialog 對話 3

Celia and Kurt are browsing in the "new releases?section at Blockbuster.

莎莉亞和科特在百視達裡正在瀏覽新片區。

C   : See anything you want to watch?

莎莉亞 : 有你想看的嗎？

K   : Not yet. You?

科特   : 沒有，你呢？

C   : Well … There is this French movie, here…

莎莉亞 : 嗯…這裡有部法國片，這裡…。

K   : No way. I don't feel like watching anything with subtitles.

科特   : 不要，我不想看任何有字幕的電影。

C   : Excuse me?! All the kung fu movies you like to watch have subtitles!

莎莉亞 :什麼話？所有你喜歡看的功夫電影都有字幕啊！

K   : Yeah so what?

科特   : 那又怎樣？

Useful Sentences 範例句型

Ever since he was a kid, Fredrick had been interested in space travel.

當費德瑞克還是小孩的時候，就對太空旅行相當有興趣了。

Tristan ran into his brother at the mall, so they went shopping together.

瑞斯坦在商場遇見他的哥哥，所以他們就一起去購物。

Alex wasn't paying attention while he was driving, which is why he ended up causing an accident.

亞歷士開車時並不專心，所以才會出車禍。

Morris didn't feel like studying, so he went out and played basketball instead.

莫理斯並沒心情用功，所以他跑出去打棒球。

Vocabulary 單字片語

☑ nightclub	夜店
☑ catch something	得到
☑ sold out	賣完
☑ midnight	午夜
☑ video	錄影帶
☑ new releases	新片
☑ subtitles	字幕

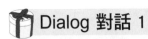
🎁 Dialog 對話 1

Grant and Megan are leaving the movie theater.
格蘭和梅格正要離開電影院。

G   : So, what did you think?
格蘭 : 嗯，你覺得如何？

M   : Thumbs down, way down.
梅格 : 不好看。

G   : Really? I enjoyed it!
格蘭 : 真的嗎？我覺得還不錯呢！

M   : Well, maybe if you'd ever read the original play
        you'd understand. This production was terrible.
梅格 : 呃，如果你看讀過原著你就會知道，這部片製作得
        很差。

G   : Well, I thought the acting was terrific.
格蘭 : 這個嘛，我覺得演得很好。

231

M : Oh, the acting was good. I just have a problem with the way the movie was edited and directed. It was like a first-year film student was in charge!

梅格 : 喔，演員演技是很好的，我只是對於電影的編排與導演的方式有意見，感覺就像電影系一年級學生導的作品般不成熟。

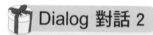 Dialog 對話 2

Kurt and Celia have finished watching their DVD.
科特和莎莉亞已經看完他們的 DVD。

C : So, what's the verdict?
莎莉亞 : 你覺得怎樣？

K : I liked it. The plot was surprising.
科特 : 我喜歡，情節很令人驚訝。

C : Wasn't it? I never saw it coming!
莎莉亞 : 可不是嘛？我根本猜不出下一步是什麼。

K : And the acting wasn't bad, either.
科特 : 而且演技也不賴。

C : Not bad?! That's the understatement of the year!
莎莉亞 : 還不賴？人家的年度評語可不只這樣呢。

K　　　: Oh, yeah! The lead actor just won an Academy award!

科特　 : 喔，對！主角剛剛贏得奧斯卡金像獎。

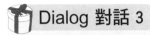 Dialog 對話 3

Celia and Kurt both notice the clock at the same time.

莎莉亞和科特同時注意到了時間。

C　　　: Wow. It's only nine thirty! What are we going to do, now?

莎莉亞 : 哇，才九點半而已！那我們現在要做什麼？

K　　　: What do you mean? I'm going home to hit the sheets.

科特　 : 還要做什麼嗎？我要回家睡覺了！

C　　　: But it's still early!

莎莉亞 : 但是還很早啊！

K　　　: For you, maybe. But I had to wake up early today for an exam. I'm beat.

科特　 : 對你而言，可能是。但是我今天一大早就起床去考試，我累了。

C　　　: So that's it? You're calling it a night?

莎莉亞 : 所以就這樣囉？這樣就結束了？

K : Sorry, Celia. I'm exhausted.

科特 : 對不起，莎莉亞，我真的精疲力盡了。

Useful Sentences 範例句型

Becca could see an argument with her boyfriend coming if they kept talking about the fact that she didn't want to go to the dance with him.

> 貝卡知道，假如她跟她男朋友繼續討論，為何她不跟他去跳舞，小倆口間必定會發生口角。

Saying Michael Jordan was an OK basketball player was the understatement of the year!

> 說麥可‧喬丹只是個還不錯的籃球員，真是年度最不入流的評語。

After hiking all the way up the mountain, Malcolm was beat.

> 健行到山頂後，麥肯實在是累掛了。

Eric called it a night and went home to sleep.

> 艾瑞克把工作告一段落，回家睡覺去。

Vocabulary 單字片語

☑ **humbs up/down** 　　　　　　　好的／遜的

☑ **original** 　　　　　　　　　　原著

☑ **production** 　　　　　　　　　製作

☑ **terrific** 　　　　　　　　　　很棒的

☑ **edit** 　　　　　　　　　　　　編劇

☑ **direct** 　　　　　　　　　　　導演

☑ **verdict** 　　　　　　　　　　見解

☑ **plot** 　　　　　　　　　　　　劇情

☑ **be in charge** 　　　　　　　　負責

MEMO

....

....

....

....

....

....

....

....

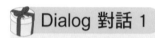 Dialog 對話 1

Celia is still interested in having fun, so she calls her friend, Matt.

莎莉亞還是想要找些樂子，所以她打給她的朋友麥特。

C : Hey, Matt! It's Celia!

莎莉亞 : 嗨，麥特！我是莎莉亞。

M : Long time no see! What's up?

麥特 : 好久不見！有什麼好玩的？

C : Not much. That's why I'm calling!

莎莉亞 : 並沒有，這也是我打電話來的原因！

M : I get it! Well, I'm about to go meet up with some of my friends, downtown.

麥特 : 了解！這個嘛，我正要去城裡跟一些朋友會合。

C : Where are you going?

莎莉亞 : 你們要去到哪裡？

M : To a nightclub called Liquid. And you're welcome
to come along, if you like!

麥特 : 去一家叫「烈酒」的夜店，如果你願意的話，歡迎你
一起來！

 Dialog 對話 2

*Celia lines up outside the nightclub. After a
while, she reaches the front of the line.*

莎莉亞在夜店外面排隊，過一會兒後，總算輪到她了。

B : ID, please.
吧員 : 身分證，謝謝！

C : Here you go.
莎莉亞 : 在這裡。

B : What year were you born in?
吧員 : 你幾年次的？

C : 1981. What's the cover charge?
莎莉亞 : 1981 年，入場費多少錢？

B : It costs twenty dollars to get in.
吧員 : 進場要二十元。

C : That's not cheap! Thanks.
莎莉亞 : 真貴！，謝了。

B : Have a good time.

吧員 : 祝你玩得愉快玩得開心點。

 Dialog 對話 3

Celia can't see her friends at the bar. She decides to go get a drink from the bartender.

莎莉亞在吧台找不到她朋友，她決定跟酒保要一杯飲料。

C : Can I have a beer, please.

莎莉亞 : 請給我一瓶啤酒。

B : Sorry, you'll have to speak louder! The music is too loud and I can't hear you!

吧員 : 不好意思，請你說大聲一點！音樂太大聲，我聽不到你說什麼！

C : A beer! I'll have a bottle of beer, please.

莎莉亞 : 啤酒！請給我一瓶啤酒。

B : Sure thing! Coming right up.

吧員 : 沒問題！馬上來。

C : How much do I owe you?

莎莉亞 : 多少錢？

B : That'll be seven dollars.

吧員 : 七塊錢。

C	: Here's eight. And you can keep the change!
莎莉亞	: 這裡是八塊錢，不用找了！

B	: Thanks for the tip!
吧員	: 謝謝你的小費！

Useful Sentences 範例句型

Alfred said, "Oh, I get it!" after his teacher explained how to slove the math problem.

當老師向艾佛德講解完這個數學題目後，艾佛德說「我懂了！」。

Hanna was born in 1980, and her younger sister in 1984.

漢娜出生在 1980 年，她妹妹則出生在 1984 年。

To get into a restricted movie, you must be at least eighteen years old.

你必須年滿十八歲，才能看限制級電影。

The waiter told the couple that their order was coming right up.

服務生跟這對夫妻說他們點的東西馬上來。

Vocabulary 單字片語

☑	downtown	市中心；鬧區
☑	be welcome	受歡迎的
☑	reach	達到
☑	ID	身分證
☑	cover charge	入場費
☑	bar	吧台
☑	bartender	酒保
☑	owe	欠
☑	bottle of something	一瓶
☑	tip	小費

MEMO

At a CD Store
在唱片行

 Dialog 對話 1

The next day, Celia meets up with Kurt to go shopping.

隔天，莎莉亞找科特去購物。

K : So, how was the rest of your night, you crazy party-animal?

科特 ：那麼你昨晚過的如何啊？你這愛玩的傢伙。

C : Great! I went out to a new night club downtown.

莎莉亞 ：太讚了！我去城裡一家新的夜店玩。

K : Which one?

科特 ：哪一家？

C : It's called Liquid. The music was awesome, which is why I want to go to the music store before we start looking around the clothing boutiques. I want to try to find some of the CDs the DJ was playing yesterday.

莎莉亞 ：「烈酒」俱樂部。音樂很棒，這也是為什麼我想在逛服裝店之前先去逛唱片行，我想要找一些昨晚 DJ 放的音樂。

K　　　: Great. There's a CD that I want to pick up, too! Let's go!

科特　　: 太好了，我也正好想買張 CD，一起去吧！

 Dialog 對話 2

Celia and Kurt are in the music store.
莎莉亞和科特在唱片行裡。

K　　　: So, what do you want, anyway?

科特　　: 那你到底想要找什麼呢？

C　　　: Well, that's the problem. I can't remember what I heard, but it wasn't like the DJ was announcing the names of the artists as he was spinning!

莎莉亞　: 呃，問得好，我不記得我聽到的，昨晚 DJ 在播放時好像也沒有公佈歌名或是歌手名。

K　　　: What kind of music was it, then? Pop? Rock?

科特　　: 是哪一種類型的音樂？流行？搖滾？

C　　　: More like hip-hop and R&B.

莎莉亞　: 比較像是嘻哈和節奏藍調。

K　　　: Then we should head to the R&B section. Luckily, this music store has listening posts, so you can preview the CDs before you buy them.

科特　　: 那我們應該到節奏藍調區域，幸好這家唱片行有試聽機，在買之前你可以先聽聽看。

 Dialog 對話 3

Celia and Kurt are getting ready to make their purchases.

莎莉亞和科特已經準備好要結帳了。

K　　　: Did you find everything you were looking for?

科特　　：你有找到你要的嗎？

C　　　: Yep. You?

莎莉亞 ：有啊，你呢？

K　　　: Almost. I saw a few CDs that I've been after, so I'll buy those. But the store is sold out of the one I really wanted.

科特　　：算有吧，我有找到一些滿喜歡的，所以我買了它們，不過我最想要的已經賣完了。

C　　　: So shall we leave? We've still got a lot of shopping left to do this afternoon.

莎莉亞 ：那我們可以走了嗎？還有很多地方要逛呢。

K　　　: I'm leaving with so many more CDs than I intended to buy, I don't know if I can afford any more shopping.

科特　　：我已經買了超過預期數量的 CD，因此可能沒錢再逛下去囉。

243

C　　　: Kurt, don't worry! Anyone can afford window shopping.

莎莉亞 ：科特！別擔心！逛街也可以不用花半毛錢。

Useful Sentences 範例句型

How are you feeling, anyway? You don't look well.

還好嗎？你看起來臉色不太好。

At the department store, the sisters headed for the cosmetics department.

姊妹們走向百貨公司的化妝品專櫃。

James used his credit card to make a purchase.

詹姆斯用他的信用卡結帳。

Lily was happy that the sale was on, because then she could afford to buy the dress she'd been after.

麗莉很高興舉辦了大特賣，這樣她就可以買下她喜歡的衣服了。

Vocabulary 單字片語

☑	party animal	派對狂
☑	awesome	驚人的
☑	boutique	時裝店
☑	DJ	放音樂的人
☑	announce	宣布
☑	spin	旋轉
☑	pop	流行
☑	rock	搖滾
☑	hip-hop	嘻哈
☑	R&B	搖滾藍調
☑	listening post	試聽機
☑	preview	預覽
☑	window shopping	只逛不買

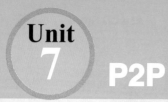

Unit 7 P2P

資源分享

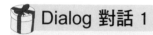 Dialog 對話 1

Kurt and Celia have gone back to Kurt's dorm room to listen to the CDs they bought, and Kurt switches on his computer.

科特和莎莉亞回到科特的宿舍,聽他們買的 CD,科特打開了他的電腦。

C : What are you up to, an end-of-term essay?

莎莉亞 :你要做什麼,期末報告嗎?

K : Not exactly. I still really want that CD that the store was sold out of. So I'm going to try to find it online.

科特 :不是啦,我還是很想要那一張已經賣完的 CD,所以我想在網路上找找看。

C : You're going to order it?

莎莉亞 :你要訂購嗎?

K : Not exactly. I'm going to do a P2P search.

科特 :不一定,我想做一些 P2P 的搜尋。

C : P2P? Is that the name of the band?

莎莉亞 :P2P? 是一個樂團的名字嗎?

K   : Nope. It's computer-speak for"peer-to-peer."It means that I can search other people's computers for information I want.

科特 : 不是,是「資源分享」的電腦術語,意思是我可以搜尋別人電腦裡我想要的資訊。

🎁 Dialog 對話 2

Kurt is searching for the music he wants.
科特正在搜尋他要的音樂。

C   : I get it. So you can exchange information in the form of music files?

莎莉亞 : 我懂了,這樣你就可以跟人家交換音樂檔囉?

K   : Or picture files, or text...anything, really.

科特 : 圖片檔,或是文件檔⋯⋯說真的,什麼都可以。

C   : Then how do you pay for the music you get?

莎莉亞 : 那你要怎麼付錢?

K   : You don't. It's free.

科特 : 不用,是免費的。

C   : But the artists who make the music–don't they get anything?

莎莉亞 : 那些歌手呢,也沒得到任何報償嗎?

K　　　: Nope, not a dime.

科特　　: 沒有，一點也沒有。

 Dialog 對話 3

Celia is getting angry.

莎莉亞開始生氣。

C　　　: Kurt, what you're doing is stealing!

莎莉亞 : 科特，你這樣簡直就是土匪！

K　　　: No, what I'm doing is sharing.

科特　　: 不是，我只是在分享。

C　　　: You mean people can upload files from your computer, too?

莎莉亞 : 你的意思是說別人也可以從你的電腦上傳檔案囉？

K　　　: That's right. As they say, it's a game of give and take.

科特　　: 對啊，就像大家說的，這只是個給予和接受的遊戲。

C　　　: Or in the case of P2P music exchanges, a game of take. I'm ashamed of you, Kurt.

莎莉亞 : 你的意思是，交換音樂只是個接受的遊戲，我真為你感到羞恥，科特。

K　　　: Alright, alright. I won't get the CD through P2P. I'll just wait for it to come out in the stores.

科特　　: 好啦！好啦！我不會從 P2P 得到這張專輯，我會等它進貨再買。

Useful Sentences 範例句型

Terry didn't have a dime and had to ask his parents for some money.

泰瑞一毛錢都沒了，因此必須跟他父母要錢。

Brandon asked his friends if they wanted to play a quick game of basketball.

布蘭登問他的朋友是否想打個籃球。

To have a successful relationship requires a willingness to give and take.

一段成功的感情需要雙方都樂於接受與付出。

Mrs. Green was ashamed of her daughter for failing the test.

格蘭太太因為女兒考試考糟，而為她感到羞恥。

Vocabulary 單字片語

☑	switch on	打開
☑	end-of-term	期末
☑	essay	論文
☑	online	上線
☑	order	訂購
☑	P2P (peer-to-peer)	資源分享
☑	search	搜尋
☑	exchange	交換
☑	upload	上傳

MEMO

....

....

....

....

....

....

....

....

Unit 8

Video Games

電玩

 Track-48

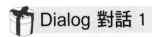 Dialog 對話 1

Celia is still steaming and won't talk to Kurt, so he starts playing a game on his computer.

莎莉亞還在對科特生氣而並且不跟他說話，所以他開始玩他的電腦遊戲。

C : What's that? A war game?

莎莉亞 ：那是什麼？戰爭遊戲嗎？

K : Yeah, it's really good. The object of the game is to destroy the enemy world.

科特 ：對，這個真的很好玩，遊戲的主題是要摧毀敵人的世界。

C : So it's a violent game. Nice.

莎莉亞 ：所以這是個暴力的遊戲囉，不錯嘛。

K : It's a game of strategy! Give it a chance; it's a lot of fun. You may like it.

科特 ：只是個戰略遊戲，試試看嘛，很好玩的，你也許會喜歡。

C : I don't think so. I don't like that kind of entertainment. But I'm not surprised you do.

莎莉亞 ：你這種個性的人會喜歡這個，我沒話説，不過我沒興趣。

K : Whew, Celia. Maybe we'd better not hang out any longer this afternoon.

科特 ：喂，莎莉亞，我看我們今天下午還是不要在一起的好。

C : Fine by me. See you.

莎莉亞 ：正合我意。再見！

K : Whatever.

科特 ：隨便你。

 Dialog 對話 2

Kurt has been playing his computer game for a few hours when the phone rings.
科特繼續玩電動玩了幾個小時，直到電話響了。

K : Yes?

科特 ：喂？

M : Hey, Kurt. It's Megan. What's up?

梅格 ：嗨，科特，我是梅格，你在做什麼？

K　　：I'm in the middle of something.

科特　：在做事。

M　　：A computer game, no doubt. I was wondering if you wanted to hang out?

梅格　：不用猜，一定是在打電動。你想不想出來晃晃？

K　　：Um. Maybe later. I'm almost finished with this level. If I can just beat this one guy...

科特　：呃，晚點吧，我就快要破關了，如果我可以擊敗這傢伙……

M　　：Alright, if you're too busy to hang out, I understand. I just wanted to tell you that my brother lent me his X-box for the weekend.

梅格　：好吧，如果你忙到不能出來，我可以體諒。我只是要告訴你，我哥哥這週末要借我 X-box 遊戲機。

K　　：X-box? I'll be right over!

科特　：X-box？我馬上過去！

 Dialog 對話 3

Kurt and Megan are playing against each other in a video game.

科特和梅格正在對打電動。

K　　：Take that! And that! Pow! Game over!

科特　：接招！還有這招！啪！遊戲結束了！

M　　 : You win, again. I give up.
梅格　 :你又贏了，我放棄。

K　　 : Come on, one more round!
科特　 :別這樣啦，再打一回嘛！

M　　 : No, I'm exhausted. We've been playing all night long. Time for me to turn in. But I'll tell you what.
梅格　 :不要，我累爆了。我們已經打了整晚了，我要睡覺了，不然這樣吧。

K　　 : What?
科特　 :哪樣？

M　　 : If you promise to take really good care of it, you can borrow the X-box for the night.
梅格　 :如果你答應好好保管，X-box 遊戲機就借你一整晚。

K　　 : Really? I think I've died and gone to heaven!
科特　 :真的嗎？我真是樂到上天堂！

Useful Sentences 範例句型

Mr. Lin told his son to give the new town they had moved to a chance.

林先生希望他兒子給他們的新家一個機會。

Neil was in the middle of a phone conversation when the doorbell rang.

尼爾講電話講到一半時，門鈴響了。

When Jim asked Ben for help, Ben said he'd be right over.

當吉姆請求班的幫忙時，他說他馬上趕到。

Vocabulary 單字片語

☑ turn in (go to bed)	去睡覺
☑ be steaming	生氣
☑ object of a game	遊戲主題
☑ destroy	摧毀
☑ enemy	敵人
☑ violent	暴力的
☑ strategy	戰略
☑ whew	喂（不滿的語氣詞）
☑ level	關卡；級數
☑ pow	啪
☑ round	回合

Dialog 對話 1

Grant and Helen are spending a quiet night at his place. They have just finished dinner.
海倫決定在格蘭家共度一個平靜的夜晚，他們剛吃完飯。

G : So, what do you want to do tonight? Go see a movie? Rent a video?

格蘭 : 你今晚想要做什麼？去看電影嗎？還是租錄影帶？

H : Actually, I'd rather just watch TV. There's a special that I want to see.

海倫 : 說真的，我想看電視，今晚有個特別節目我滿想看的。

G : A made-for-TV movie?

格蘭 : 是電視影集嗎？

H : No, a documentary on the Second World War.

海倫 : 不，是第二次世界大戰的紀錄片。

G : What time does it start?

格蘭 : 幾點開始？

H : Around nine, I think. Can you pass me the TV guide?

海倫 : 我想應該是九點，你可以把電視節目表傳給我嗎？

 Dialog 對話 2

Helen is looking through the TV guide while Grant channel surfs.

海倫在看電視節目表，格蘭則隨意轉台。

G　　: See it?

格蘭　:找到了嗎？

H　　: I'm looking...Channel twelve. But it doesn't start
　　　until nine thirty.

海倫　:我正在找……第 12 台，不過九點半才開始。

G　　: What's on before then?

格蘭　:那之前演什麼？

H　　: Not much. A few re-runs, a game show...

海倫　:沒什麼，一些重播的節目，一個遊戲節目…

G　　: Never mind! Look what's on TV now!

格蘭　:沒關係！先看看現在有什麼節目！

H　　: Survivor! I love this show!

海倫　:「生存遊戲」！我喜歡這個節目！

257

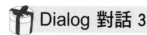 Dialog 對話 3

It's ten o'clock, and Survivor is just ending.
十點了，「生存遊戲」才剛播完。

H : Ah, where did the time go? We've missed the beginning of the documentary! Channel twelve, quick!

海倫 : 啊，現在幾點了？我們錯過了紀錄片的開頭，轉到 12 台，快！

G : I don't have the remote control!

格蘭 : 遙控器不在我這！

H : Where is it? Where is it?

海倫 : 在哪裡？在哪裡？

G : Hey, if you don't calm down, I'm going to vote you off the island!

格蘭 : 如果你不冷靜下來，我要請你下台囉！

H : I found it. Now, shh!

海倫 : 找到了，現在安靜！

Useful Sentences 範例句型

Claude passed the meat to his father at the dinner table.

　　用餐時，克勞德把肉傳給他爸爸。

Carl was channel surfing because there was nothing on TV that interested him.

卡爾正在隨意轉台，因為現在他沒什麼特別想看的節目。

Andrea asked her sister what was on TV at ten o'clock.

安德魯問他姊姊十點電視在演什麼。

There wasn't much that the veterinarian could do for the sick dog.

獸醫對這隻生病的狗已經無能為力了。

Vocabulary 單字片語

☑ tube		電視螢幕
☑ special		特別
☑ made-for-TV movie		電視影集
☑ documentary		紀錄片
☑ TV guide		電視節目表
☑ channel		頻道
☑ re-run		重播
☑ game show		遊戲節目
☑ remote control		遙控器
☑ vote		投票

Dialog 對話 1

Grant and Helen have finished watching the documentary.

格蘭和海倫看完了紀錄片。

G   : Yawn! Time for bed!

格蘭 ：哈～啊，該睡覺了！

H   : Not just yet. I want to get a bite to eat. I'm starving!

海倫 ：還早啦！我想吃點東西，我餓死了！

G   : You must have a hollow leg! You ate seconds at dinnertime.

格蘭 ：你的胃是無底洞啊！你晚餐已經吃兩頓了。

H   : I have a healthy appetite. Now let's see what's in your fridge.

海倫 ：我有健康的好胃口。現在我們來看看你冰箱裡有什麼。

G   : I'm afraid you're going to be disappointed...

格蘭 ：我怕你會失望喔。

H   : There's little else in here but mayonnaise and bananas? What kind of diet are you on anyway?

海倫   ：除了美奶滋和香蕉以外什麼都沒有？你在實行哪一門節食法啊？

G   : Don't blame me! Bachelors aren't known for their healthy eating habits.

格蘭   ：別責怪我！大學生對健康飲食是沒半點概念的。

 Dialog 對話 2

Helen has decided that a trip to the night market is in order.

海倫決定去夜市一趟。

G   : Do you want me to come with you?

格蘭   ：你要我跟你去嗎？

H   : Of course! It's not safe for a girl to be walking the streets alone at this hour.

海倫   ：當然，這個時候讓一個女生走在巷子裡是很危險的。

G   : Alright, let me get my coat...What was that?!

格蘭   ：好啦，我拿一下外套，什麼聲音？

H   : My stomach growling.

海倫   ：我肚子叫的聲音。

G   : You must be really hungry! OK, I'm ready to go.

格蘭   ：你一定很餓！好了，我可以出發了。

H   : Let's roll!

海倫   ：我們走吧！

 Dialog 對話 3

Helen and Grant are at the night market. Helen has just wolfed down some noodles.

海倫和格蘭在夜市裡，海倫剛狼吞虎嚥完一碗麵。

G   : Satisfied?

格蘭   ：飽了嗎？

H   : Not yet. I still want a mango ice, and an ice tea.

海倫   ：還沒，我還想要一碗芒果冰和冰紅茶。

G   : Mmm. I could go for an ice tea, too. There's a great vendor just a few stalls away.

格蘭   ：嗯，我也想喝杯冰紅茶，過去幾家店就有個不錯的攤子。

H   : I'm glad you know your way around here. Lead the way. Wait!

海倫   ：我很高興你對這附近很熟，帶路吧。等等！

G   : What is it?

格蘭   ：怎麼了？

H : Stop here for just a second. This vendor's fried chicken looks delicious!

海倫 : 在這裡停一下，這家店的炸雞看起來很好吃！

After the ball game, we stopped by a fast food restaurant for a bite to eat.

打完球後，我們到速食店吃點東西。

There was little else to eat at the barbeque but hotdogs and hamburgers, so the vegetarians left quite hungry.

這家燒烤店除了熱狗和漢堡外沒有別的了，所以這位素食者只能飢腸轆轆地離開。

There was nobody to blame for the fact that they couldn't go camping: the weather was simply too cold.

露營取消不是任何人的錯，只怪天氣太冷了。

Diana was so hungry that everyone in the class could hear her stomach growling!

黛安娜實在太餓了，教室裡的每一個人都聽見她肚子在叫。

Vocabulary 單字片語

☑	yawn	打哈欠
☑	starve	飢餓
☑	have a hollow leg	食量很大
☑	eat/have seconds	吃第二次
☑	appetite	胃口
☑	disappoint	失望
☑	mayonnaise	美乃滋
☑	bachelor	大學生
☑	wolf something down	狼吞虎嚥
☑	satisfy	滿足
☑	vendor	小攤販
☑	stall	商家

國家圖書館出版品預行編目資料

可以馬上學會的超強英語口說課/蘇盈
盈, 珊朵拉合著. -- 新北市：哈福企業,
2020.11
　　面；　　公分. -- (; 67)

ISBN 978-986-99161-6-5(平裝附光碟片)
1.英語 2.會話

805.188　　　　　　　　　　109016666

英語系列：67

書名 / 可以馬上學會的超強英語口說課
合著 / 蘇盈盈・卡拉卡
出版單位 / 哈福企業有限公司
責任編輯 / Mary Chang
封面設計 / Lin Lin House
內文排版 / Co Co
出版者 / 哈福企業有限公司
地址 / 新北市板橋區五權街 16 號
封面內文圖 / 取材自 Shutterstock

email／welike8686@Gmail.com
電話／(02) 2808-4587
傳真／(02) 2808-6245
出版日期／2020 年 11 月
台幣定價／330 元
港幣定價／110 元
Copyright © Harward Enterprise Co., Ltd

總代理／采舍國際有限公司
地址／新北市中和區中山路二段 366 巷 10 號 3 樓
電話／(02) 8245-8786
傳真／(02) 8245-8718

Original Copyright © EDS Culture Co., Ltd.

哈福